St Cuthbert's
Wild School for Boys

Ingrid Skeels

To Joe and Eve with love

Contact ingridskeels@gmail.com

Design: Ruth Bateson
ruth@grounded-design.co.uk

One

The day Jack first heard about St Cuthbert's Wild School for Boys began as any other. He woke early, tried not to think of *certain things*, turned on his torch and reached for the book at the end of his bed: a collection of twenty different Master Mazes, each more twisted and tortuous than the last. Jack was on number 11, a mass of writhing, knotted snakes he had to find a way between. Tricky! But he was getting there. And there was still an hour before *the dreaded…* He clipped his torch onto an old tie he had turned into a headband, allowing maximum light and freedom for both hands, and set his mind to tackling the snakes.

"Jack?"

An hour later Jack's mum came stumbling into the room, still in pyjamas, her hair scruffy and her eyes not properly seeing yet. "Come on! Time to get up – we're going to be late for school!"

Jack turned his head so the torch shone directly into his mum's face and she winced at the light. *Like a great all-seeing eye*, he thought. *A Cyclops! Only better, because I've got three eyes, and…*

"Jack!" His mum trod on a bit of Lego and booted it crossly out of the way. "Turn that thing off and get up, will you? And you Ellie."

Ellie was Jack's sister. She slept below him on the bottom bunk and was different in nearly every way. For a start she was a girl. She was young and he was old (well, old-er) and she was little and he was tall. But also, she had straight yellow hair and his was curly red. She woke up late in the mornings and he woke up early. She loved school and he found it boring. And – the big one – she didn't remember their dad and he did, though he didn't like to go on about that one.

If he had to sum her up, Ellie was small, different and annoying. But she was also funny and had gone along with all of Jack's younger games, including The Great Inspector Drew, Spies, Cowboys and that *brilliant* monkey game he had invented... Plus, she did let him pretend the bedroom was his. He was grateful for that.

Jack's mum drew back the green curtains and light zoomed into their room. Ellie whined, like Zombie their cat, and burrowed under the covers.

What was it with his family and light? They were... *what was it*? Hydrophobic? Claustrophobic? No, that was being scared of small spaces. What was the word for *fear of light*? All the *fear of* words came from Ancient Greek, Jack knew that, so *lightophobic* definitely wouldn't be right.

If only he had a copy of the Complete Reverse Dictionary! The CRD was the latest thing on Jack's list of things that needed to be invented: a book where, instead of looking up words to find their meaning, you look up meanings to find the word you need! So obvious! He was going to develop the idea and make a lot of money. He just needed to start writing everything down. The papers were somewhere at the end of his bed...

"Jack! Did you hear me? Get up! Ellie you come down with me."

Abandoning his search for the CRD, Jack jumped down from the top bunk, landing in a crouch. He pulled on his clothes – cotton, denim, cotton, sweatshirt, and then sock, sock. Lying on the carpet for a moment to yank up his second sock, he caught sight of the space under the bed; a place he totally forgot existed until every so often, at ground level, he would find himself peering into it. Amongst the fluff he identified his old watch – *so that's where it is!* – several marbles, a tiny Lego space cart he had made ages ago and a chocolate coin. *A chocolate coin! From last year?* He looked around for a long sweeping implement to reach and retrieve the lost treasures and, very possibly, to eat one of them...

"Jack! Are you coming down or not?"

The clear out would have to wait and he would probably forget again. He took some more socks out of his chest of drawers and arranged them in a rough arrow shape, pointing under the bed, and then raced downstairs.

In the kitchen, Ellie was already dressed and eating the huge bowl of cereal she ate every morning: a mountain of Cornflakes with two Weetabix on top.

How could she consume all that and still be so small? *An enormous tapeworm* Jack had long ago decided, *living in her gut, feeding off the food she eats.* He'd seen a picture of one once – thin and white – with the chilling label:

The longest tapeworm to be pulled from a human body was 37 feet – 11.27 metres – long!

Ugh! But how *did* you pull one from the human body? And how did it get there to start with?

"Toast, Jack?"

"Oh, um, okay."

He always had toast with jam or, if there was time, inventions of his own involving fried eggs and tomatoes, maple syrup and raisins, or various other *Jack Specials*.

His mum passed a plate across, saying: "Come on, get a move on!" And then, more quietly: "Now, what else do I need to remember?" She was always talking to herself like this, under her breath. At one point, Jack had even wondered if that was where the word '*mum*ble' had come from.

But right now he wasn't listening. He was smearing butter on his toast remembering how, when he was little, his mum would turn it into a flat house, cutting windows and a door, and then use jam to paint the front. *How babyish was that!* And yet, he kind of wanted to try it again, experimentally...

"Have we got any peanut butter, Mum, or something thick?"

"Thick? No...why? Anyway there isn't time." She and Ellie were already pulling on their coats. "You'll have to bring that with you. We're already late."

"Okay, okay..."

School time. Again. Another day. Why did the weekends and holidays go so quickly and the school days come round so often? Why did school have to involve so much... school?

And it seemed to Jack, as he shoved his feet into his trainers, grabbed his bag, put the hood of his coat onto his head and yanked his scooter out of the corner where it was tangled with the hoover, that it was all he ever did really. He had no idea – not a single clue – that today would be the last day in quite a while that 'school time' would mean anything like his particular school. Or, in fact, like any school he had ever heard of before.

~ ~ ~ ~ ~

Jack's school was ten minutes walk from his house at the end of a long road of shops. Not too far, but there were so many big and busy roads to cross that he wasn't allowed to go on his own. No children were. Instead, he had to scoot down with his mum, weaving in between her and Ellie and gliding ahead of them where he could along the grey and littered street.

"Jack! Look out! You're too near the road!" His mum grabbed his coat as a lorry laboured past, honking and throwing up clouds of grit into their faces.

Jack sighed. She was always panicking that he was going to get hit by a car or a lorry, or that he would bash into someone else. It was like nothing and no one was safe.

"Okay okay…"

He slowed down so he was gliding along beside them, his scooter needing only the slightest expert touch of his trainer on the pavement to keep going. Vans and cars roared past noisily, sometimes with the pale face of one of his school friends peering from the window.

And the litter and dust swirled and eddied around them.

At the end of the shops, across the road and round the corner were the school gates where by now, crowds of children wearing the green Kerry Road school sweatshirt had merged from every direction to go into school.

Jack searched the sea of heads for Max, his friend, who always wore a red baseball cap. It was no use looking at anything but heads, as the playground was so small and busy and everyone was wearing the same.

He thought again how helpful it would be to develop some kind of Personalised Child Identification Tag for schools with uniforms. Each tag would be individual, perhaps something you could wear on your head, or stick to your back, so you could spot your friend from far away. He personally didn't need a PCIT as he had curly red hair and everyone always saw him immediately including, unfortunately, the teachers. But he would be happy to develop the concept for others and of course wear one to show willing. He fancied a golden eagle, wings spread to full majestic width, right across his back, with the head turned to one side and the curved predator's beak just resting on his shoulder...

"Bye love!" His mum touched his arm. "I'm taking Ellie in now. Pass me your scooter and have a good day."

"Mum... that's not going to happen." He moved out of the way to let some younger girls pass.

"Oh Jack. Not this again." A familiar worried look appeared on his mum's face. "Can't you be a bit more positive?"

Jack sighed. "Can't it be a bit more interesting?"

A loud clanging noise started up from the other side of the playground as the red faced Headmaster, Mr Clipper, rang the bell for school and swept his gaze

8

around the playground. Jack's mum squeezed his arm and set off towards the younger classes with Ellie, lugging his scooter with her.

Jack turned slowly towards his classroom door.

~   ~   ~   ~   ~

Perhaps if Jack had known that this was his last day at Kerry Road Primary School, before heading off on the adventure of his life, he might have enjoyed it more, or at least paid attention more, or even just savoured the finality of it... But he didn't, so he couldn't, and the day passed much as any other.

First he had Literacy. Their *learning objective* (that's what his teacher called it anyway) was to revise the use of adjectives and adverbs. They had to use as many good ones as they could in a timed piece of writing, making sure that they planned it all first on a bit of paper and that the beginning and ending of the story were interesting.

Jack found it a strange *conundrum* (oh how he liked that word!) that an activity that kept telling him to be interesting was so boring to do! And he got told off several times for whispering to Max about the Complete Reverse Dictionary.

Next was numeracy. Their *learning objective* was to understand fractions: dividing whole numbers into equal sized bits. Jack got told off for messing around with his watch and putting pencil shavings into little piles.

Then it was lunchtime. Jack and Max got told off for climbing on the low wall that divided the playground ("Not safe!") and for swinging from the low branch of

9

the one tree they had there ("Dangerous!") and then for loads of other things.

Jack's school was strict and seemed to get more strict after every School Inspection they had. There were so many rules now! No running, no bikes and no scooters; no conkers, no marbles, no football cards or any other kind of cards or things to swap; no open-toed sandals (a girl in Year Two had got a chair leg on her toe and had to go to hospital); no chocolate, crisps, nuts, fizzy drinks; no sweet corn, peas or rice (choking!); no climbing, skipping, hopscotch, holding hands or playing in threes (too many arguments); no touching any soil; and no shouting, screaming or singing (some of the songs could be rude). Oh, and no football. Or any ball game. And they never got to play with the younger children.

Jack only ever glimpsed Ellie across the dividing wall, walking around in her red coat with her friends. She looked happier than him.

Lunch itself was a rush, as always. There were too many children, not enough time and the food wasn't very nice. There wasn't a kitchen big enough to cook in properly at Jack's school, so the food arrived in huge trays to be heated up. And it never seemed to really taste of anything. Once, just once, the cook had insisted on making her own biscuits in the small school oven, especially for Easter.

Jack still remembered the melty crumbliness of that biscuit.

In the afternoon Jack's teacher, Mrs Wirksworth, told them about the interesting new project they would be starting.

"Our theme is Rome!" she announced, as she rifled through a huge pile of papers. "But to save time we will combine it with another of our learning objectives this term, so in PE we will be starting with Roman dance."

Roman dance. *Roman dance??* Did the Romans dance? How did they? How do we know how they did? Jack really wanted to ask these questions, but knew better than to try. There never seemed to be time for Mrs Wirksworth to explain anything that wasn't on her list of what they were supposed to learn. And almost every question that *she* asked *him*, she already knew the answer to. It seemed she just wanted to hear that answer back.

And none of the projects ever ended up being as exciting as he thought they would be: Light and Dark, Sailing Craft, the Tudors... They all sounded so good but in the end just involved things the teachers wanted you to say and do, so they could tick them off in their book. They weren't *really* about exploring light and dark, or sailing boats. Not how Jack would do it anyway. He'd want to grope about in the dark, pretending to be blind. Or sail in a real boat. Or at least make something float on a pond. Or even just in the sink...

So all in all, Jack had stopped bothering with school and questions long ago. It was easier just to do what they wanted you to do. Or ignore it.

Which is what he did now, turning his attention to the extremely interesting experiment he was conducting on his desk. A ruler, balanced on a rubber, tipped down one end and then the other. But if he got the rubber exactly – *exactly, mind* – in the middle, the ruler stayed perfectly in a straight line. He had found balancing point! It must have a name! What could it be? Another great example of the need for the amazing Complete Reverse Dictionary!

"Jack Everett! Are you listening to anything I say?" Mrs Wirksworth was staring at him in her usual frazzled way. She beckoned him over to her desk. "I would like to see you and your mum up here after school," she continued ominously. "We have to do something about this terrible lack of attention."

Oh dear. Not good. Not good at all.

Two

"The thing is," Jack's mum was saying to Mrs Wirksworth an hour later in the same classroom, while Ellie looked at books and Jack pretended to. "The thing is, at home, Jack is really clever and interested in loads of things. Like the other week, he invented a complete code alphabet! You know, giving each letter of the alphabet a different symbol? A was a cross and B was an eye and C was... what was C in your alphabet again Jack?"

"A dagger." Jack didn't look up from his book.

"That was it, a dagger... And all the letters had symbols, right the way to Z. He copied it out for Max and they've been writing to each other in code ever since!"

Mrs Wirksworth nodded her head and smiled brightly in a way that Jack recognised. It meant *I know I need to look like I'm interested in what you're telling me, but there are things I need to be telling you!* He saw that smile often in school.

"Jack is a bright boy," Mrs Wirksworth continued now. "He could do well. But he just won't settle down. He doesn't listen, he talks all the time, he fidgets, he messes about and he doesn't put effort into his work.

He's just not applying himself and he's distracting others, including Max. And he always looks so bored!"

"We-ll…" Jack's mum glanced across at him.

"He really should be much further along with his numeracy and literacy by now."

"I'm sure if we could just find a way to make him more interested…" Jack's mum began.

There was a silence. Mrs Wirksworth closed her eyes and, for a moment, looked almost sad. She took a deep breath. "I have thirty children in this class, Mrs Everett, and I have to constantly monitor the progress of every single one. I have a huge list of learning objectives to get through, endless tests to prepare the children for, and our school is due for another inspection any day now. Mr Clipper is determined that we will do better this time. There is simply not the time or space for me to do what you suggest. Jack has to start fitting in and getting on, and he needs to do it soon. Or he's going to get labelled as 'difficult'. And that wont be good when he goes up to secondary school!"

There was a thud from over in the reading corner as Jack dropped the book he was looking at.

"Jack?" said Mrs Wirksworth, in a different, brighter tone. "What about we set up a Behaviour Chart? Every day you come to school and manage to really listen and learn, I'll give you a golden arrow sticker. And when you get enough, I'll give you a reward. A sweet maybe! What do you think?"

Jack looked at his mum's face.

"Okay, okay," he said wearily.

~ ~ ~ ~ ~

"Mum, do you remember when I was little, I said that trees were like broccoli?"

Half an hour later Jack, his mum and Ellie were sitting in a café waiting to be served. Jack's mum was still looking worried and he was trying to cheer her up. Talking about when he was little usually did the trick. It made him feel better too. It gave him such a *whole* feeling. This time, though, he noticed that his mum barely smiled. He tried again.

"Do you remember when I put the washing up gloves on my feet to be a penguin?"

They often came to a café for a drink and a cake when there was something to celebrate or, as in this case, something serious to discuss (though cake was never offered on those occasions, he noticed). It seemed there were some things that just needed a cup of tea his mum didn't have to make herself. And it stopped things turning into an argument, which they often did.

This particular café was strange, very strange, and quite a new addition to the Kerry Road shops. Jack didn't know it yet but it was also somewhere that was about to change his life forever.

"It's good we came here, Mum," he said, looking round, already the bad feeling of school slipping away. Cafes were always coming and going along this bit of Kerry Road but Jack had been noticing this one for ages now. For weeks, the windows had been blacked out with paper so no one could see in, which made you really want to, and there had been lots of comings and goings of delivery vans and builders and packages. Then, a few days ago, some huge green plants and leaves had appeared in the windows, so thick you still could hardly see in, which made it even more intriguing. Yesterday, a big sign had gone up – **Café Amazon** – and today, as they looked for somewhere to go, a notice on the door said **Open!**

So here they were. And inside, the café was even more strange! The huge plants and leaves that nearly blocked out the light from the window were also growing all around the room. There were even some creepers hanging down from the ceiling, giving the whole place a weird green light. And attached to the walls were strange wooden things – Jack couldn't make out if they were weapons or musical instruments – and some black and white photographs showing brown skinned people with not a lot on. Jack wasn't sure if the people of Kerry Road would want to look at pictures of naked people in a café, even if they were foreign and only in olden day black and white. But it would be interesting to observe!

In the background, instead of music, there was a soundtrack of strange and wonderful birds, cooing and squawking and chattering in a bird language that definitely was not English. It felt peaceful and exciting at the same time and Jack smiled as he moved a bit of creeper that was hanging down too close to his head.

"It's like Max's room in The Wild Things book, remember? When it's half changed into the woods?"

His mum smiled a little bit and at that moment a man appeared from the back of the café, wiping his hands on the front of a big white apron. He was quite old, about Jack's grandad's age, and he was a bit brown skinned too, but only from the sun. He had a dusty, happy feeling about him and he made Jack think of *far away*.

"Welcome to Café Amazon! How do you like the jungle?"

"*Cool!*" Jack grinned.

"The rainforest! It's one of my Things, you know. Now, what can I get you?" he looked from one to the other of them and smiled.

"What is there?" asked Jack.

"Is it drinks you want or food or both?"

"Just drinks," said Jack's mum, firmly.

"Well, I have some wonderful juices, made from the little known fruits of the Amazon. There's Guarana berry or Acai."

Jack thought for a moment. "Guarana please."

"Can I have the Acky one?" said Ellie.

"Um... Just a cup of tea for me please. Normal tea that is."

"Certainly Madam. Coming right up." And he left them.

The three sat in silence for a while, fiddling with a teaspoon (Ellie), the salt pot (Jack) and her nails (his mum), while the noise of something being whizzed up somewhere out of sight joined the cacophony of the birds. Jack was about to wander off and get a better look at the weapons/musical instruments – *maybe they're both? In some situations, it might actually be extremely useful –* when his mum reminded him of why they were there.

"So, Jack, what on earth are we going to do?" She stared at him for a moment and, when he didn't answer, added, "Is there another problem with school I don't know about? Are you being bullied? Are you worried about something? Is it still about Dad?"

Jack said nothing.

"Why can't you settle down like Mrs Wirksworth said and apply yourself to your work? I thought we'd agreed you were going to try harder with your reading and writing?"

Jack sighed. "It's none of that," he said finally. "I just don't like it."

"But why? Ellie likes it there, and Max seems to get on okay."

"I don't know…" Jack felt a familiar tight feeling in his chest. He *hated* being compared to others. "It's just, there are too many rules and tests and stuff. It's boring! Learning is boring!" He put down the salt pot, hard. "I just can't see the point of any of it and I don't want any golden stupid arrows or sweets. How old does she think I am?"

"I know Jack. And I do understand what you're saying, I really do." His mum put her hand on his own. "But you have to go to school, love, whether you find it interesting or not. It's the law. And I'm certainly not teaching you at home. We'd both go mad!"

"But I'm no good at any of it! I probably never will be!"

"Excuse me…"

None of them had noticed the café man who had appeared beside them carrying a tray of drinks: one purple, one rather murky orange-green, and one teacup. "If I may be so bold as to interrupt your discussion…" He looked at Jack's mum and then placed the purple drink in front of Jack and the other by Ellie. "I wonder if I might have the solution to your problem."

Jack's mum looked at him blankly. "I'm not quite sure that…"

"But first," he continued, placing the cup of tea in front of her, "a little test, if I may."

18

Jack's mum started to make a polite but doubtful kind of noise, but the man turned to Jack who was staring at him with interest.

"You see, many, many years ago," he began, "I left these shores to travel the world, to seek my fortune, if you like. I was a young man, and quite naïve in many ways. But I was full of the spirit of adventure and I wanted to see and hear and smell and taste and touch new places. So, leaving with only a small amount of money, some spare clothes and a few provisions, I set off, planning to work as I went to earn my food and lodging. Where I travelled and what I did is a long story. And each place, each night, each day, is another hundred stories that we don't have time for here..."

Jack's mum looked like she was going to say something at this point, but luckily the man carried on.

"Eventually, I found my way to the edge of the Amazon Rain Forest. And you cannot imagine, my friend, until you have been there yourself, the sight and feel of that great forest, that great river and all the life teeming within. Imagine for a moment the vastness of the desert: the silence, the dryness, the seeming emptiness... and then, if you can, try to imagine its complete opposite, and you will get close to what I was facing. At that moment I had to decide whether to carry on with my journey, into that great noisy wildness. Or to turn away..."

"Excuse me!" Jack's mum sounded a bit more definite now. "I'm sorry to interrupt you, and it does sound a wonderful story, but..."

"Mum – please! Let him finish!" Jack turned back to the man. "What happened? Did you go in? What did you see? What was it like?"

"Aha!" the man slapped a hand on his apron side. "You've passed the test, my boy!"

"Test...?" Jack and his mum looked at each other and then stared blankly at the man. *What was he talking about?*

"Just my little way of finding out," he continued, still smiling. "Don't worry, I can tell you my travel tales another time. But I see that you, my dear boy, still have within you the spark of interest to seek out and question and experience and learn. With so many children I see it is already dead... But in you, it is very much alive and well!" He turned to Jack's now rather astonished mum and bowed his head slightly.

"Let me introduce myself Madam. My name is Rupert Woolacroft and I wonder whether this" – he held up a finger as if to pause the world while he pulled from his apron pocket a dark blue pamphlet covered with ornate gold writing – "just might be the answer to your problem."

All three of them leant forward to read, in blazing, golden, curling script:

St Cuthbert's Wild School For Boys

Three

For the hundredth time that weekend, Jack thought of the dark blue pamphlet. Where was it? Why couldn't he look at it? What did it say?

In Café Amazon, after only a moment, Jack's mum had taken it and put it firmly in her bag, as if she knew that once opened, it would be hard to close. She had politely thanked Rupert Woolacroft for his kind suggestion and made it very clear that they wanted to finish their drinks. In private. Rupert Woolacroft was very gracious.

"Of course," he said, leaving them at once.

Later, he held open the door and passed a small card to Jack's mum. "My number. In case you want to find out more."

And now here Jack was on a Sunday afternoon, with only homework ahead of him. Ellie was out at a birthday party, his mum was ironing and he was on the sofa, bored. He drummed his hands against the arm.

"Can I go on the computer?" There was this cool game that he and Max had discovered, where you shoot zombies and each one dies a different kind of weirdo death: dissolving, turning into dribble, going green and shrinking, desiccating (that meant going dry, like his mum's cooking); exploding... He was on Level Six but he was sure he could get to Level Ten if...

"No way Jack. You've been on it all morning." His mum reached for a shirt from the ironing pile and shook it out. "I'm sick of the sight of you staring at that screen and banging away on the keyboard. Find something else to do."

"Telly then?" he asked, hopefully.

"No! That's no different!"

"It's TOTALLY different!" Jack sometimes could not believe the small understanding his mum had of modern technology. She only seemed to grasp the very surface functions of anything.

"It's still a screen you're staring at," she said, smoothing the shirt onto the ironing board. "You know what I mean. Go and do something else."

"There's isn't anything else! I'm bored of everything we've got." Jack could hear the whine creeping into his voice. The whine she didn't like. The whine that made her cross. But it was true: there *was* nothing else to do!

"Well go in the garden and get some fresh air! Play football!" She started ironing, pressing the iron down hard.

"Our garden's tiny! And it's concrete! And you can't play football on your own."

"Well think of something else then!" His mum was getting really annoyed now. He could feel it. "Look at Ellie! She doesn't mope around saying she's bored. She just gets on with it."

"Ellie!" Jack kicked the floor. '*Ellie!* Ellie's little! And she's a girl. And maybe I got on with it when I was her age. What I'm saying is I'M BORED NOW!"

"Jack!" His mum banged the iron down hard. "When I was your age, I didn't have half the things you have and I played all day long. Stop being such a pain!"

"Yeah?" he shouted, leaping to his feet. "Were you allowed out to play in the streets? Yes! Were you allowed to the park on your own? Yes! Could you go and call for your friends and do what you wanted? Yes! You've told me hundreds of times about when you were little, but I'm not allowed to do any of it! I'm sick of only going to the park with you and I'm sick of our road and I'm sick of everything!" And he kicked the end of the sofa with his trainered foot, hard, leaving a dusty smear.

"Don't you DARE do that!" his mum yelled, red and fiery.

But it was true and she knew it and she sat down heavily in the old armchair and put her curly head in her hands. "The thing is Jack," she said in a weary voice, looking up. "Life often isn't fair. Times have changed since I was little. I just don't feel ready to let you go where you want. Anything could happen. You have to learn to do stuff where you are. Or at Max's house."

Jack groaned and covered his face. In the darkness he felt there was no way out of this boredom and it would possibly never end; an endless, airless tunnel of brown boredom, with only computer games and sports clubs to break it up. And even if she did let him out, what would he do? Where would he go? There was just traffic, gritty streets, parks with no children...

He just couldn't escape the feeling that there was something wrong, something missing, something more that people weren't telling him...

"Anyway," Jack's mum said suddenly, in a different tone. "Shouldn't you be doing your homework?"

"Agghhh!!!" He fell to the floor in frustration. *This is how an animal feels when it's trapped!* he thought. And he saw, for a moment, the lions in the zoo: eating, sleeping and, when they understood, roaring and pacing their cage.

~ ~ ~ ~ ~

Half an hour later Jack was lying on the floor, pencil in hand, revision worksheet by his side. Ellie, back from the party, was playing upstairs. This is what he had to do:

Adjective and adverb recap!! Complete the 10 questions. Fill in the blank spaces with your own good describing words. Remember to notice if you are describing an action or a thing:

1. **The _____ man went _____ into the _____ garden.**
2. **The _____ bird flew _____ across the _____ sky.**
3. **The _____ children laughed _____.**
4. **A _____ mouse...**

Jack was on number two and so far he had written:

1. **The *happy* man went *quickly* into the *big* garden.**
2. **The *happy* bird flew...**

But he had lost interest a while ago. Instead, he was sketching a design for a new weapon, the weapon to end all weapons and alter hand to hand combat for ever: a long straight, jagged blade which curved gently at the end; a mixture of sword, saw and scythe. He would call it the Super S.S.S and...

"Jack! What *on earth* are you doing?" His mum appeared behind him, carrying a shopping bag. "You're meant to be doing your homework!"

"Well I've started it!"

"Let me have a look. Oh Jack..." she put down her bag. "This isn't very good!"

"What's wrong with it?"

"Well you say all the time you like words and you've just put 'happy' both times. This is your chance to show Mrs Wirksworth what you can do! This is exactly what she was talking about on Friday Jack and it's just lazy!"

"I'm NOT lazy!" Jack threw down his pencil and turned on his back, his arm over his eyes, a tight feeling squeezing his chest.

"Well try harder then! Show her!"

"Show her what?!"

"Show her what good words you know! Show her that you're clever and that you can do it! Try and get good marks! Otherwise it's like she says, they'll think you're no good and that's going to make everything harder when you move schools."

"I – DON"T – CARE!" Jack hit the floor with his fists. "You don't get it, do you? She's not interested in me or what's in my head. And I don't want to do it. It's BORING!"

He leapt up, slammed out of the room and rushed to the bedroom where Ellie, frozen mid-game, stared at him in alarm.

"GET OUT OF MY ROOM!!!!" he yelled.

She went, double quick, leaving him alone and angry and miserable. And very possibly crying.

~ ~ ~ ~ ~

A long while later, when the anger had gone and Jack was feeling drained and miserable, his mum knocked on the door and came in. She was carrying a plate with his favourite sandwich invention: white bread, cheese, mango chutney, cucumber and mayonnaise. She put it down on the chest of drawers. It was perfect timing: any earlier and he would have thrown his pillow at the door; any later and he would have got too hungry and been forced to go downstairs – a humiliating defeat.

"Sorry," said his mum.

"Sorry," said Jack, and they hugged each other tightly, his mum wanting to carry it on longer than he did, as usual. And for a moment he really smelt his mum, the way you do when you hug people and you're squashed against their clothes and maybe a bit of their skin and hair. They smell so much of themselves like that, but with a bit of what they've been doing too: cooking tea, sleeping, or being outdoors. His mum smelt of strawberries always, from her shampoo, and a deep homely, woolly smell that was just *her*. His mum.

You can even smell of the night Jack thought. His dad used to, when it was winter and he came home after work in the dark.

"Hey – what's that?" Over his mum's shoulder, Jack caught sight of something dark blue with a flash of gold, under the sandwich plate.

"Oh – that!" His mum un-hugged herself. "I don't know if it will do any good looking at it, or if it's just a waste of time. But I don't want you to be unhappy at school Jack, or unhappy here. I just thought that maybe

26

we should at least have a look at the Wild School leaflet and... well, just see if it gives us any ideas."

Wild School... Even the name thrilled Jack!

"But I'm telling you now, I can't afford to pay for a private school. And I don't want you leaving home."

"Okay okay!"

Jack leapt down from his bunk and together they knelt on the floor to look at the pamphlet. The gold letters on the front danced and shone back at them and his mum opened the cover and carefully folded it back. Inside, there were just two pages of thick, creamy coloured paper with dark blue writing and coloured photographs. On Jack's side, it said:

Rules of the School

1. *No Targets*
2. *No Worksheets*
3. *No Tests*
4. *Only essential Health and Safety Rules*

Jack looked up. "What's Health and Safety?"

"Rules to keep you from having accidents. You know, like at Kerry Road."

"Oh."

And then:

5. *No computers, phones, hand-held devices or screens of any kind*

Oh! Not so cool.

Underneath there was more writing, which his mum was now reading aloud. Jack heard the words *broad curriculum... physical development... outdoors... learning through experience...* but his attention was caught by something much more interesting: the photographs. There were two of them. The top one showed a group of boys walking together across a green lawn. They were filthy, covered in mud, laughing and smiling, as if after some kind of extreme rugby or football game, which they had won, or at least massively enjoyed. *As if... but not quite.* Jack noticed that they weren't wearing sports kit, just their own slightly torn and muddy clothes.

The second one was even more intriguing. It was a big photograph that took up nearly half of the second page and it showed a huge, beautiful old house with a drive leading up to it, meadows and trees stretching away on either side.

"Is that the school?" It didn't look like a school. It looked like a mansion.

"Hang on Jack. I'm still reading... But yes, that must be the school."

"*Cool!*"

"A lot of private schools are in amazing old buildings but you have to pay a lot of money to go to them and they exclude so many people... Oh, actually... Look at that! That's interesting..." His mum pointed to some writing under the photograph:

Education at St Cuthbert's Wild School for Boys is at no cost to boys and their families, but all boys must be specifically recommended to us by one of the members of our Board.

"Perhaps I should phone Rupert Woolacroft and find out more..." his mum's voice was thoughtful. "After all, it can't do any harm just to get information. Shall I do that? Yes, I'll do it now." And she left the room, still *mum*bling to herself.

But Jack wasn't listening. He was still looking at the photograph of the house, at something he could see – or thought he could see – in the trees.

Quickly he went to the wooden desk that he shared with Ellie and yanked open one of the drawers on his side, rummaging through a mixture of swimming certificates, diagrams of monsters, and here and there a fossil, a crystal, a sweet, until he found what he was looking for: his super-power magnifying glass. He rushed back to the brochure on the floor and examined the photograph again, through the lens.

It *was* what he had thought! There, in one of the trees at the side of the meadow, was a wooden construction, a very complex kind of tree house that with normal vision had just looked like part of the tree – if it wasn't for the flag that Jack had spotted sticking out above it. He adjusted the lens. Yes, there was the flag... it had something on it but it was too faint to see. It looked like a kind of bird.

And there, poking out at the side of the tree house, visible only with Jack's extra strong lens, was the head of a boy, hair on end, his face wearing an expression of what could only be described as pure and utter glee.

Four

Jack sat in the car and watched the grey blocks of the city become empty suburbs become a long neat village and then fields, stretching away on either side of the road, open and free. The afternoon light was golden amber and the air smelt faintly of smoke.

"Bonfire!" shouted Ellie.

And then there was silence as each gazed out of the window, lost in their own thoughts and the drive westwards. Jack watched the fields, broken only once by a big flash of river.

How quickly things had moved since the weekend! Was it only two days ago that they had knelt and looked at the blue and gold pamphlet and his mum had phoned Rupert Woolacroft? She had gone to talk to him at Café Amazon that very evening, leaving Jack and Ellie with Mrs Watson next door, an old lady with a big tin of custard cream biscuits and milky cups of tea to dunk them in. When she came back, ages later, his mum was serious and thoughtful.

"You know Jack," she said, as she poured a very green liquid into three bowls and put them on the table.

"I've been thinking."

Jack, heavy with custard creams, looked uneasily at the soup and saw Ellie eying it with the same expression of dread.

"And what I'm wondering is whether St Cuthbert's really might be something you could try. Just for a few weeks, if you would like to."

"Really?"

This was not at all what Jack had expected. He looked closely at his mum.

"It just sounds," she said, stirring her spoon round and round her soup, "like a place where boys can maybe start to enjoy school again. They only take people for a term I think, or a year at the most..." And here she looked up suddenly, "Though don't for a second think you would go for a term, Jack! I am thinking for a few weeks maximum! I wouldn't want you away from home for any longer. But..." (stir, stir, thoughtfully), "it might help you with school. It might just change things for you at Kerry Road. And we wouldn't even have to pay for it, not if Rupert recommends us. What do you think?"

"Are you serious?" Jack eyed his mum through the steam of his soup. Rupert Woolacroft must have answered all of her questions and smoothed out all of her worries. And she was someone with *a lot* of worries.

"I am serious." She sipped a spoonful of green. "But only if you want to. Now, eat up and I'll tell you more after."

Jack looked at her in amazement. His stomach was churning with custard creams. "I don't think I can eat anymore," he said.

"Me too," said Ellie quickly, putting down her spoon. "I'm excited too."

~   ~   ~   ~   ~

As it turned out, Jack's mum didn't need to tell him much more before he made his decision. After tea, she rummaged in her bag and pulled out a ragged sheet of paper. It was a kit list for St Cuthbert's: all the things a boy would need to go to the school. This is what he read:

St Cuthbert's Wild School For Boys: Kit List

- Clothes for hot weather
- Clothes for cold weather
- Waterproof coat
- Wellington boots
- Waterproof trousers
- Sleeping Bag
- Torch (ideally head torch)

Cool!

- Swiss army knife (if you have one)

Yes! I finally get to use Dad's!

- Tin opener
- Swimming things
- Wet suit

Wet suit??!

- Bike, if you wish

Bike!!! Yes!!! I never get to go on mine!

- *Compass*
- *Ruler*
- *Ink pen and range of nibs*

"What's a *nib*, Mum?"

"It's the metal bit at the end of a proper ink pen. The bit you write with."

"Oh."

- *Sharp HB pencils*

If he needed any more persuading (which he didn't), it was this final item that totally convinced Jack. He loved sharp pencils. They were the best things to design with, to invent with, to write with. They made you feel so precise and neat and like you were doing something properly. Blunt pencils were rubbish, just rubbish. It seemed easier to get everything wrong and messy with a blunt pencil.

But not everyone understood these facts! And his constant sharpening of pencils at school often got him into trouble. Now, finally, here was someone who understood. Who agreed even!

"So what do you think, Jack?"

"Well..." He looked at his mum with the curly hair and he looked at Ellie who was playing with Zombie. He knew he would miss them... a lot... And yet, he just had a feeling he had to try this.

"I want to do it!"

"Good." His mum hugged him. She seemed pleased, in a mixed kind of way. "I'll go and talk to Mr Clipper tomorrow."

But that night, Jack noticed that she tried for a longer hug when he went to bed and he worried that she was sad as well as glad.

"Do you remember when I used to call soldiers *shoulders*?" he said.

For a moment he thought he had made matters worse but then his mum said, "I do Jack. But you're growing up now and this is all part of you making your own way in the world and trying something new. And I am going to help you do it."

In bed, trying to be extra quiet for Ellie, Jack lay awake for a while, letting everything that was happening to him settle in his head. Soon he heard a rustle from below.

"Jack?"

"What?"

"Why *do* you want to go to the Wild School?"

In the dark, with Ellie asking so straightly, the question seemed much bigger, but also somehow clearer. "Because" he said, "it makes me feel excited. And our school doesn't."

"Oh."

A while later, after more rustling, she said: "But what about your friends?"

What about his friends? Well, Max would be here when he came back! He didn't see Liam and Stan out of school anyway, except at clubs. And anyway, he might even make new friends...

"I'll be okay."

"But... what about us? Will you be all right without us?"

Jack thought again. Would he? How could he know? He'd never done it before.

"I'll be alright," he said. And then, realising that what Ellie was really worried about was whether *she* would be all right without *him*, he said: "But I'll miss you Ellie. Will you write to me?"

"I will," Ellie said. "But some of the letters still face the wrong way."

And then they must have fallen asleep because that was all he remembered.

~ ~ ~ ~ ~

Now, here he was, sitting in the back of the car, driving to St Cuthbert's Wild School for Boys! In the boot was his suitcase, crammed full of the stuff on the list. Jack thought happily of his NEW head torch; the purple sleeping bag and Swiss army knife that were his dad's; his new ink pen *with a nib;* and the very, very sharpened pencils that his mum had almost stopped him packing because she thought they were dangerous.

No bike, sadly. His mum hadn't let him take it, of course. So the new, lightweight, mountain bike that he had got for birthday and Christmas combined, after begging and pleading, was still at home and hardly used.

And that was it! He didn't have a compass because they weren't sure if the list meant the small metal tool that helps you to draw a perfect circle, or the little clock thing that tells you how to find north, south, east or west. It could have been either, so in the end they got neither.

But that was okay. *Wasn't it?* Jack was beginning to feel nervous now. And he was worried about what he was wearing too. At the last minute, they had checked the kit list again and seen, in very small writing at the bottom, a note that said:

There is no school uniform at St Cuthbert's Wild School for Boys and we do not wish parents to go to any extra cost, so please bring the uniform from your current school.

"That's a bit odd!" his mum had said.

It *was* a bit odd! But he had pulled on his Kerry Road sweatshirt just as they were setting off and now he really wanted to take it off. He wanted to be as neutral as possible until he knew what everyone else would be wearing. He sank a little further into his seat.

"Are we nearly there?" he asked, half hoping half dreading that they were. They had turned off the motorway a while ago and were now driving along a busy road, with fields on one side and low, wooded hills on the other.

"There should be a small road any time now on the right," said his mum, slowing down a bit and glancing at the instructions on the seat next to her. She had been quiet for most of the journey, as had Ellie, who usually sang and chatted all the time in the car but was instead fiddling with something she had hidden in her pocket.

It was strange when people went quiet and kind of disappeared into their minds like that, Jack thought. It was like you lost them for a while. It reminded him of one time, years ago, when he was little and couldn't get to sleep and his mum had come and sat by his bed and stroked his head. With his eyes closed and her hand on his forehead, he had felt sure of her full attention. But when he had opened his eyes – just a tiny bit – to see her, she wasn't even looking at him! She was staring into space, seeing something far away or long ago or deep inside. Definitely not the room and definitely not him. And Jack had felt that she was beyond him, somehow, and it had made him feel kind of lonely.

But now, now that he was older, he understood that people had their own minds, their own feelings – just as he did, and even Ellie did.

"Oops… This is it!" Jack's mum made a swift bend to the right and now they were driving along a much smaller, quieter road, with high grass sides to it and trees at the top, so that they drove in and out of flashes of sun and patches of shadow. The trees were turning brown and gold but there was still much more green than he was used to.

"Look out for a sign to St Cuthbert's sometime soon on the left, Jack."

He watched the side of the road, his eyes glued to the bank ahead of the car. But it was Ellie who shouted five minutes later. Or was it five hours? It seemed like forever. "A sign! A sign!"

And there it was: a dark blue sign with curly, gold writing, just ahead of them as the grass banks disappeared and a huge meadow appeared on Jack's side.

"St Cuthbert's Wild School for Boys…" Ellie sounded out very slowly, as the car slowed down.

Almost immediately there was the driveway: a simple open gateway, a straight white road stretching across the meadow and, at the end of it, the great golden square of a house that Jack recognised instantly from the photograph.

"We're here," he breathed. And his voice sounded shaky, even to him.

"Yes – here we go," said his mum. She turned the car into the driveway and drove slowly up towards the school.

Five

The final drive up towards the school was terrible. Jack felt like he would die of nerves. He tried to look towards the big trees at the edges of the meadow. Was there a tree house? He couldn't see anything. Not a stick, a flag, nothing. But he was having trouble concentrating on anything. A flock of birds – never mind butterflies – wheeled and dived inside him and his hands were sticky and awkward. What should he do with them? It was like he'd never had hands before. They were just in the way.

A mad impulse to run leapt in Jack's gut but he was trapped by the seatbelt. All he could do was say, in a slightly strangled voice, "I'm not sure that..."

But it was okay. He knew, and his mum knew, and Ellie knew – because of the Climbing Wall Incident last year – that this nervy feeling was just something to get through.

It's not a bad thing, the Climbing Wall Man had said at the time. *It's a sign that you're doing something big and daring for you. And it's a sign that there might be danger. So when you do feel nervous, weigh up how much you want to do the thing and how much danger really is involved. Then, if you decide to go ahead, just take a deep breath right down into your nerves...* Jack cringed as he saw again the restless queue, the impatient feet, the craning necks. *...And go ahead. Try! Most often, you'll do the thing you're scared of, and enjoy it, maybe even be good at it! But if not, at least you tried...*

And Jack had done it! He'd mustered up the courage to climb shakily to the top, hit the bell and abseil down. Then he'd told everyone he wanted to do it again.

So right now, he breathed deeply into his nerves and assessed the situation: (1) He wanted to try St Cuthbert's; (2) he would feel disappointed if they went home; (3) there was no danger; and (4) it was too late! The car was stopping, his mum was opening the door and a large smiling woman was coming down the steps towards them.

"Mrs Hopewell?" Jack's mum was already out of the car and offering to shake hands.

"And you must be Mrs Everett," the woman replied, grasping Jack's mum's hand. She turned to Jack and Ellie who had unstrapped themselves from the car and were standing, crumpled and unsure, nearby.

"I'm the school housekeeper. I organise all the sleeping and cooking and home things at St Cuthbert's. You must be Jack... And who's this?"

"This is Ellie," said Jack's mum.

"Well, come in, come in..."

They followed her up the wide steps, through a huge front door and into a large, tiled hallway. A great staircase rose from the middle and then curved out of sight.

"This is Sarah, the school secretary." Mrs Hopewell pointed through a half open doorway to the left, where a young woman with a high ponytail was working on a very old computer. She turned and smiled.

"Hiya!" she said.

"And this," said Mrs Hopewell, pointing to the door on the other side, "is Mr Bonham – the Head Master's – room. He should be here..."

"...Any minute now!" a booming deep voice replied as a man – a smallish man with straight, floppy grey hair and bright blue eyes – appeared from the back of the hallway with his arms spread wide, followed closely by a small brown sausage dog on little tappy legs.

"Mrs Everett... Jack... and Ellie isn't it? Welcome to St Cuthbert's Wild School for Boys!"

He opened the wide panelled door of his study and gestured them inside. "This is Zoe by the way," he added, as the dog pit pat patted between their legs and shot into the room. One by one they followed her in.

~ ~ ~ ~ ~

Jack looked round Mr Bonham's study with interest. It was nothing at all like Mr Clipper's room! His was small and bare with shelves of coloured folders and nothing much on the walls, just some photos of Kerry Road children from years ago getting certificates and a huge chart measuring *All Test Results And Standards in This School*. There was a big bar graph, a multi-coloured pie chart and a jaggedy line to which Mr Clipper added a new bit every single day, in different coloured pens. Above this line it read *Attendance Figures,* in large letters. Everyone knew it measured how many children turned up for school every day, and how many were ill, or on holiday or just not there. The line certainly zigzagged up and down a bit and if you were late for registration or forgot to tell the school office you were going to the dentist, a few minutes later Mr Clipper would be at his chart, crossly putting right the latest bit of zig or zag and muttering to himself.

And it seemed to Jack that in all his time at Kerry Road, if he had to say what had been the most important thing to the Headmaster, it would have been those charts and that zigging zagging line.

Which is why now, standing in Mr Bonham's room, Jack was so interested. It was completely different! The room was big and light with pale blue walls and criss-crossed wooden shelves, full of books of every colour, shape and size.

And even more interesting was what else was in the room because, apart from Mr Bonham's huge wooden desk, the two chairs facing it and a little flowery cushion nest for Zoe, most of the study was taken up with different sized glass cases, like in a museum. And in the glass cases – and in fact on every surface that Jack could see, including on the floor – were hundreds, thousands! – of fossils: tiny, small, medium and even a few that were really huge! There were jagged broken bits and round wholes; flat shiny bits and some that looked like they'd just come out of the earth. There was grey rock, black rock, brown rock and red rock. There was an enormous stone slab in the corner with faint markings, like drawings, all over it. And loads of the round, snaky fossil – *What was it called again? Ammonite!* – in bits, and in amazing, perfect coils.

"Wow!" Jack looked around, trying to take it all in.

"My fossils!" Mr Bonham said happily, clearing papers from his desk. "Rather a passion of mine. One of *my Things*. I've been collecting them since I was a boy of your age. Do have a seat all of you and make yourselves comfortable."

Jack's mum sat down on one of the chairs and immediately jumped up in alarm, moving a rather spikey looking fossil from the seat, and then pulled Ellie onto her lap. Jack headed for the other chair but was quickly drawn to the big stone slab. It was covered with spidery stems and faint fan shaped leaves, like an old cave drawing he had once seen.

"Jack!" said his mum. "Sit down please."

"Don't worry Mrs Everett," said Mr Bonham, smiling. "It's good to see he has an interest in the world around him. At St Cuthbert's we like to encourage that. We believe that learning comes from that sense of wonder at everything around us. Quite impressive, aren't they Jack? *Ginkgo Huttoni*... or fossilised leaves, to you and me, from the Ginkgo tree, crushed flat between layers of soil some 167 – 164 million years ago. A time we now refer to as the Middle Jurassic Bathonian Stage. Or, more commonly, *when dinosaurs roamed the earth*!

Of course, the Gingko tree only grows in China and Japan today, but I found that very fossil in Yorkshire, and dinosaurs probably munched the very next leaves to those ones there..."

Jack stared at the slab, seeing great slobbering jaws tearing leaves from the tattered branches of the tree, leaving just a few to cling on and survive, somehow, until today...

"So!" Mr Bonham began again. "You've come to join us for a short while, Jack. And I'm sure my good friend

Rupert Woolacroft, a very interesting man, has filled you in on lots of things about St Cuthbert's." He smiled again at Jack's mum.

"Well…" she began to say.

"As for you Jack, you'll find out most through simply being here and doing things, and I do think that's the best way. Experience is always stronger than being told everything. There's nothing like picking a stinging nettle to teach you not to pick stinging nettles, that's what I always say!"

Mr Bonham laughed. He really did seem to relish the idea of people stinging their fingers in order to learn not to do it again.

"Still," he went on, serious again. "The boys are in lessons until two o clock, which means we have a little time before I find your room mates…"

Room mates!

"…to show you round. So, a few facts!" He clasped his hands together and looked up at the ceiling, perhaps deciding what to say. Ellie crept over to pet Zoe and Jack looked straight ahead, waiting.

"St Cuthbert's is a very old school," he began. "A few hundred years old in fact. And it has always been a very good school, although it has changed a lot over the years. At one point, you know, and for a very long time, it was only the wealthiest families who could afford to send their boys here. At another point, the entire school was closed down for many years and this whole building…" he spread out his arms "…was just empty and forgotten and full of bats."

"Bats – cool! How many?"

"Jack!" His mum frowned at him.

"No, no, that's right. It was rather interesting actually. There must have been several hundred at least. Maybe more. Including some rather rare species, I believe. And there were spiders too of course. And all the things that come creeping and flying in when you abandon a place. Dirt, dust, leaves, mice...

Then, fifteen years ago, the building was bought and restored and St Cuthbert's was re-opened. But this time..." Mr Bonham sat up straight in his chair, his eyes bright, and lifted a finger into the air. "...This time, free to all boys who come, from all over the country, and open *especially* to boys who are sick of school and fed up of learning." His voice got louder and his eyes got brighter and he sat up straighter. He's *excited,* thought Jack.

"That is," continued Mr Bonham in his louder voice, "boys who don't see the point of school and can't be bothered to go anymore; boys who long for the weekends and the holidays to come; boys who get that heavy feeling on a Monday morning, or a Sunday night, or even every day. But...' and Jack saw his finger go higher in the air. "But, but but...! Open only to boys who, like yourself Jack, still have that spark of interest within them: to find things out, to understand things, to see and do and hear and experience more..."

Mr Bonham's hand dropped and his voice went back to normal.

"Of course," he went on, "that spark is always there in all of us, however buried. But we do have to see it exists before we can allow boys to come here, or our task would just be too difficult.

And that..." he said, looking pleased again, "is where our Board comes in. Our members pass on the boys that they come across; boys they think will benefit from what St Cuthbert's has to offer. And that is how they – and you – get to come here."

So Rupert Woolacroft is a Board member, thought Jack. *And he spotted Me!*

"You see, Jack," Mr Bonham leant forward in his chair. "At St Cuthbert's we believe lots of things about learning, but the most important thing – the one thing that I want to impress upon you now – is that we believe all boys – all people – need to find what it is in life they are interested in, what they love doing and what they are good at. The best learning will come from this, the best and happiest people, and so the best community, country and world. Do you understand what I mean?"

"Not... really," said Jack, honestly.

"Never mind. You will! You see..."

At that moment, a bell began to chime steadily, high above the study.

"Goodness!" Mr Bonham stood up and immediately Zoe stood too and tap-trotted over to his feet. "Two o' clock already! But there's usually a few minutes before they all come down. Let me pop to the office and find one of your roommates. And perhaps..." he paused at the door, "now would be a good moment to say your goodbyes?"

He smiled again and then left, quietly closing the door behind him.

Silence. Jack turned to his mum and Ellie. He had almost forgotten this bit, listening to Mr Bonham and looking at the fossils! But now that the room was quiet, he remembered with a churning thud in his belly: *this is it! I'm going to be left here!*

He swallowed, feeling suddenly small and tightly curled in on himself, like an ammonite. *Maybe this is not such a good idea...* Maybe he should just go home, even if it did mean boring Kerry Road School and never playing out. Everything seemed liquid suddenly, shimmering.

"Jack, do you not just want to come home with us?"

Something in his mum's voice made Jack blink and look at her closely. She was upset and Jack knew immediately that she was about to change her mind. And once her mind was changed, that would be it. Like the time the students next door gave him their old telly for his bedroom and his mum had said *thank you* and *yes great* and then, after a fatal delay in the students getting it to him (because it always took them ages to do anything), she changed her mind... And that was that. No telly in bedroom. Not ever. If she changed her mind now, Jack would never get a chance to try out a different school, find out about the boys and the tree house, the *essential health and safety* and, most intriguing of all, *the Wild*.

Suddenly a deep rumbling noise from above broke the silence in the room. It grew rapidly and expanded. Jack recognised it immediately as the muffled sound of chairs being scraped back, children getting to their feet, talking, laughing, shouting. A lesson was ending and free time was beginning.

And perhaps it was the sounds of that free time – the quality of the laughter, the calling and shouting as boys left the classrooms and came thundering down the stairs and crunching across the gravel outside – but quickly Jack seized the moment, before it was too late.

"No Mum! I really want to try it! I'll be fine."

Jack's mum smiled in a watery way and hugged him tightly and for too long. Then he and Ellie looked at each other.

"I made you this!" she said, finally bringing out what was in her pocket. It was a necklace made from pasta shells threaded onto some cotton. Some of the shells had globs of paint on and some were shattered. "You can wear it every day to remind you of us."

"Wow... Thanks Ellie!"

Was there really a time, even when he was small, when he had thought you could wear a pasta necklace to a new school?

"It's really good. Thank you."

"Phone when you want to Jack," his mum added. "Mr Bonham says there's one you can use any time."

"I will."

The last stray thuds sounded down the stairs and passed the study. Unseen boys were heading outside, their voices becoming fainter and fainter. At that moment, Jack heard the Headmaster's voice booming out across the hall.

"Ah, Vinnie! Not so fast. Where are Zed and Charlie?"

"Out in the woods Mr Bonham," a rather high and perky voice replied.

"Well, Jack is here. I need one of you to take him to your room and show him around."

"I'll do it!" the perky voice almost shouted. "Where is he?"

"In here, Vinnie. Come on, he's waiting."

And Jack was.

Six

"This way!" Vinnie said.

The small, freckled boy shook Jack's hand and then gestured to the wide wooden staircase, away from the study where the door was closing on his sister, mum, the Headmaster and Zoe the dog.

The boys took the stairs two at a time, the way you do when you know a staircase well. Jack did it all the time at home but now, in this new place, his stride was awkward and big. He had to keep looking at the grubby red carpet to judge his steps and keep up. From outside he could hear the distant shouts and cries of boys having fun.

"Is that your school top?" Vinnie paused on a half landing. "This is mine. We have to wear them here."

He turned round and showed Jack his grey blazer with the words St Mary's C of E Primary School written on the pocket, underneath an embroidered shield.

"Church of England," he said, seeing Jack looking at the design. On the bottom half he wore long blue shorts, two odd socks and some scruffy trainers.

"Mind you," he added, "mine's not as bad as some. Zed's is *really* bad. Wait 'til you see it. And at least we get to wear what we want on the bottom. It's the only bad thing about St C-Cuthbert's really, the uniform. Well, that and NO c-computers. But everything else is *really* good here. You'll see."

They stared at each other a moment.

"I c-can't say my c's," Vinnie said. "But I'm way better than I was. It used to be loads of letters."

Jack didn't know what to say so he just nodded.

They carried on to the top of the first flight of stairs and then they came to a great square landing. Vinnie pointed to the corridors on either side.

"This is where all the c-classrooms are and where we have our lessons and stuff. Well, when we have them, and when they're indoors."

There were lots of framed maps on the wall, some of which looked really old, but nothing else to say that this was a school as Jack knew it: no drawings or written work stapled onto coloured sugar paper; no signs from the teacher explaining what the work was trying to do.

"The library's down there too. And our c-common rooms, where we go if we want a quiet time and stuff. The bedrooms are on the next floor. There are loads of them, but ours is one of the best. Well, *we* think it is. C-come on."

And they went on up the red staircase, smaller and less grand now. Near the top, a door banged and a younger boy rushed down the stairs towards them.

"All right Ed?" asked Vinnie.

"Quick move to the side!" the boy shouted, without so much as looking at them. "I'm late for my team meeting."

"All right all right!" Vinnie said, moving, and Jack followed suit. "You'll get there. No need to knock people out of the way."

But the boy – Ed – had already thundered down the stairs. Soon they heard the door to the outside bang shut somewhere down below and then a fast, gravel-crunching sound that stopped suddenly, when his feet must have hit the grass.

"What's a team meeting?" asked Jack, as they came to the top.

"Well," Vinnie paused, his hand on the banister. "Your team is like your c-class, only better. Did you have Houses at your school? It's like that, only more fun. It's like your gang. They're c-called after bird names here."

Jack worried about causing so many 'c' words but Vinnie seemed unperturbed.

"It's all bedrooms up here," he went on, "and Mrs Hopewell's flat. She's really nice. She sort of looks after us and organises everything. Her husband died, so she likes living with us. She says she'd get lonely otherwise."

"Oh…"

Jack and Vinnie pushed through a door on the right and set off down a long corridor, with rooms opening off on either side. As they passed half-open doorways Jack glimpsed posters, muddy football socks, a big pile of comics and books on the floor, birthday cards balanced on a radiator… The next door was closed with a large sign stuck to it that read:

This room belongs to Wilf, Sam P, Angelo and Joe. Don't even think of coming in without asking (unless you're coming to tidy up, in which case, you're very welcome).

"That's Wilf's room," said Vinnie, pausing. "He's nice. He's in our team. Everyone on this side of the c-corridor is. The other side is K-kestrel and then through there is Falcon and the rooms for when you're ill."

Jack eyed Vinnie. It seemed such an effort for him to say certain words; he felt bad even listening to him. But Vinnie seemed happy, so maybe he should just ignore it? "What's our team called?" Jack asked eventually, with a rush of hot, red to his face and a tiny curl of excitement as he said the word 'our'.

"We're Eagle, the red team."

Eagle! An image flickered in Jack's mind: his Personalised Child Identification Tag! "Cool!"

"Well, this is ours." Vinnie stopped in front of the end door. Stuck on it, with yellowed Sellotape, were three pictures of faces drawn in pencil with lots of sharp detail.

"That's Charlie's work," he said, seeing Jack staring. "He's really into Art and stuff. It's one of his Things. He spends loads of time over at Studio 3. That's the Art Room. I more love sport. Specially c-cricket. Look, that one's me."

Jack studied the drawing of a small, freckle-dotted face. It definitely had something of the liveliness of Vinnie in it. The words St Mary's C of E were printed across the top and there was also a sharp copy of the shield on Vinnie's blazer.

"It's really good!" Jack peered at the detail. It really was! He looked quickly at the other two drawings: a large face with glasses that was serious and cheeky at the same time; and a sharp face with black hair that looked quite cross.

"That's Charlie and that's Zed," said Vinnie, pushing open the door and going in. "They sleep in here too."

Jack paused for a moment on the threshold of the room. Wow! It was so big! It was huge in fact, with a sloping ceiling near the window and a big window seat below. There were four beds, spread out around the room, and next to each bed a chest of drawers and a chair. There was nothing special in it – just some cricket posters around one bed and drawings around another – but the size was so impressive, especially after Jack's room at home.

"Good isn't it!" Vinnie sat down on one of the beds near the window, the one with the cricket posters round it, and bounced a little.

Jack nodded. But something felt a little strange...

It wasn't the mess. He was used to that, and in fact he felt quite reassured by the arms and legs of clothes lying around, the glass of water balanced on some books, the empty crisp packet. One of the beds was strangely neat and tidy, with nothing round it, as if the person wasn't planning on staying very long – but at least you could tell it belonged to someone.

No, it was the last bed that bothered him, the one on the other side of the window, the one that was completely bare. It was his bed of course. And there was something about the blankness of it all that made him feel weird, as if he didn't quite exist yet. And the walls, covered in dibs and dabs of white where pictures had been pulled down, perhaps even days ago; they made him think about the person before him. Where was that boy now and what was he doing? Had everyone liked him and wanted him to stay? Was he good at lots of things?

For a moment Jack felt a sharp, deep longing for his room at home. For the rickety bunk beds covered in stickers, the sheets that smelt of sleep and spilt cough mixture, for Ellie and her teddies, the fluff and the mess and the crumbs and the scattering of toys. Even for Kerry Road, where at least he knew what he was: someone who didn't concentrate and whose work wasn't very good.

"That's you," said Vinnie, pointing to the blank space.

Jack went slowly across and sat down in a sunny spot where the mattress was warm. Like Zombie his cat would have done. He stared at his shoes.

Perhaps Vinnie could see the way things were going. Perhaps he had seen it before with other new boys. Perhaps he even remembered it himself: that feeling, seesawing between excitement and fear that at low moments led to home.

"C-come on!" he cried, jumping to his feet. "Let's go and find the others. I want to show you our Den!"

~ ~ ~ ~ ~

Soon Jack and Vinnie were racing down the stairs like Ed before them and bursting through the double doors at the back of the grand hallway, their feet going at a flying crunch across the gravel.

Immediately Jack saw outbuildings and the stripy lawn of a long garden. But there was no time to look properly, just a quick shaky view as they skittered past, heading left to a wide, grassy field that stretched into the trees beyond. With a satisfying thud, their feet hit the grass and the running was quieter, apart from their panting breath.

Why were they running? What was the hurry? It seemed no matter where Jack was or what he did, this was always what adults wanted to know: *What's the hurry? What's the rush?* But – and he had thought about this a lot of times – it's not something children ask. You get an idea, a good game, someone you want to see, and the spark of it can set you flying, excitement in your chest pulling you forward faster than your legs can take you, racing to make it real.

And the only sensible question about any of that, as far as Jack could see, was why don't adults do it? *And when does it stop?*

Why, for example, does an adult never say *Come on! I want to get to work!* and start skip running down the road? And why, when they catch the first glimpse of the sea from the sand, do they not just drop everything to run down there? Or when they see their friends in the park or the street, race at top speed to see them?

These were multi-billion dollar questions all right, and ones his mum couldn't answer.

It just stops she had said, quite thoughtfully. *Bit by bit. Like when you go to school, Jack. You don't run down there, do you?*

And no, Jack had to agree, he didn't.

Right now, he ran faster, just to prove he could. He could have run faster still, easily overtaking Vinnie. But he was the New Boy. And at that thought, as they neared the trees, he faltered and slowed down.

"This way Jack!" Vinnie called, looking back through the trees.

But Jack had come to a complete standstill now. It wasn't only nerves. No, these had been overtaken – massively overtaken – by a feeling of total awe at what he could see before him. He gasped. It was like looking for a cat and finding a lion! For there, in the clearing, where he had expected – what? A little camp in the bushes?... was a truly vast old oak tree, stretching high into the sky; and on its many branches was the biggest and most amazing tree house that Jack had ever seen. Or was it houses? There were so many levels and platforms and ropes and ladders and pulleys and swings that at first, Jack didn't even register the boys that were all over it too. It was like a castle, a fort, a small village, a settlement, high up in the trees. He gazed, tilting his head back to take it all in...

"Hello!" A boy, tall and blonde, jumped down from the lowest branch in front of him and, wiping his muddied hand on his plain white shirt, held it out to Jack. "I'm Wilf. Welcome to our Den." He grinned proudly. "What do you think?"

"It's..." Jack was still looking up in wonder. "How did you do it? How did you build it?" And then, looking quickly at Wilf, "Does Mr Bonham know?"

Wilf threw back his head and laughed. "Of course! He told us to do it. It's this year's Design and Technology challenge! *Design and build a den, somewhere in the grounds of the school, and use whatever materials you can find.*"

"Or beg, borrow and steal!" called out a boy from the first platform, pulling up a basket of something on a rope.

"Well," Wilf frowned. "Not exactly steal. But we are allowed to get things from the tip. There's a massive landfill site near here. You know, where they take all the rubbish? And we can ask Alex the caretaker to go and look for stuff, or get him to take us so we can look ourselves. You find amazing things there. Charlie found a deep sea diving suit!"

"Yeah I really did!" a voice called from higher up.

Jack looked up at the tree. He began to take in the other boys above him, sitting or standing on about seven or eight platforms of different sizes and heights. Some had been working, one looked like he was reading a comic and others were just peering out between the branches. They had all stopped doing anything since Jack arrived and were staring down at him in an interested kind of way.

"It's so cool!" said Jack, after a while, looking back at Wilf and Vinnie. Both smiled proudly and a kind of pleased feeling emanated down from the tree.

"Yep!" Wilf nodded. "It's the best Den by far out of all the teams. We've been spying on them so we know. There's this tradition at St Cuthbert's that each of us, on our own, has to find the other teams' Dens and tag them with our colour. Ours is red. Most of us have done it now, so we know ours is the best!"

For the first time, Jack noticed lots of little rags of yellow and blue material tied to some of the thin, lower branches of the tree. The Eagles' Den had obviously been found by everyone. But then, it wasn't very hidden.

"That's the only downside to using the biggest tree," said Vinnie, guessing Jack's thoughts. "We're too easy to find."

"Well, so what!" said Wilf. "Ours is way better than any of the others, and way better than any tree houses before too! When was the last tree house challenge again?" he called up into the tree.

"Three years ago!" an unseen boy shouted down.

"We weren't here then," Wilf went on. "But we've seen what's left of them. We've taken all the old wood from them now. But trust me, this one is definitely the best."

Jack believed him! Could any tree house be as good as this? Even the one he had seen poking out of the trees in the picture couldn't have been anything like this.

"It's taken us weeks to get this far," Wilf said. "But now we're stuck. See that big platform half way up?"

Jack looked and saw a wide floor wedged in the fork of the largest branch and the trunk.

"We need to find a way to give it a roof, one that we can take off when we want to. We've tried with old umbrellas but there are too many gaps and they just fall off. We've tried bin bags, cut open and stuck together, but the first wind got rid of that idea..."

"We tried blankets!" a boy called from the bottom branch. "But they just got wet."

"When spring comes, the whole thing will be hidden by leaves. But right now we need some shelter for our team meetings. Anyway..." Wilf waved aside his plans, "Go up! You're an Eagle so you can go up whenever you want. There's a massive swing round the back too, over a really big drop!"

"Actually," a voice said coldly from Jack's left. "It's not worth it."

Jack turned to see a boy he hadn't noticed before, sitting on the ground a little distance away, sharpening a stick with a penknife. He was wearing a strange black cloak thing, tucked as much as possible into his trousers, and next to him on the floor was a top hat. His sharp, cool gaze met Jack's without smiling and his slightly cross pale face looked familiar.

"Well it's not!" he repeated to Wilf, who was frowning at him. "It'll be tea time soon, seeing as we have English tonight." He looked pointedly at Jack. "That's *literacy* to you. If you're coming, that is." And he went back to cutting sharp slivers of wood from his stick, slowly and deliberately, a small smile on his face.

"Of course he's coming," said Wilf, in a rather annoyed tone.

"Jack meet Zed and Zed meet Jack," said Vinnie helpfully from the side. Jack went a little closer and got ready to smile, if this boy would let him. But Zed looked only downwards.

"Delighted to meet you," he said, in a flat and decidedly un-delighted voice. And a curly sliver of wood flicked out from his stick and hit Jack's shoe.

"C-come on," said Vinnie, pulling Jack away and over to the tree. And then, more quietly, "He's all right really Jack. Just got his problems, you know."

Jack did know. He'd known lots of boys with problems. In fact, he had problems himself.

But as he set his foot on the first of the wooden footholds, nailed into the trunk of the great tree, even knowing he was going to have to share a room with Zed couldn't stop the joy of climbing up for Jack. The climbing wall was nothing compared to this! The feeling of holding onto one rough notch of wood and finding one below with your foot and pushing yourself up; of coming to the first platform and heaving yourself onto it (*like getting out of a swimming pool!*); of resting, smiling and saying hello to the boy that is there – Angelo was it? And surely that one with glasses must be

Charlie? – and then swinging onto the next branch and the platform above.

Nothing could stop the joy of climbing up and up for Jack, from one platform to the next, on branches, footholds and swinging rope ladders; and the pleasure of passing smiling boys and helping hands, until he reached the highest level. *The Crows' Nest* one of them called it. From there, he peered down through dry branches at the scene below: the smiling upturned faces of Vinnie and Wilf, the smaller trees, the green field, the big house...

A bell began to chime across the grass and he heard Wilf calling him.

"Come down Jack! It's tea time!"

He was starving, he realised. Even so, he couldn't resist gazing again at all that he could see.

Was this seriously his new school?

Seven

Mmmmm. Delicious.

Jack popped another hunk of cake in his mouth and closed his eyes with pleasure. He hoped very much that this was a sign of meals to come. Right now, on his plate, was a huge chunk of fruit-cake, dark brown and riddled with raisins and cherries; some Scotch pancakes, small golden rounds smeared with butter; and a scone, warm and crumbly, topped with a great glob of raspberry jam and another of thick yellow cream, both smearing together nicely. Much as he wanted them, Jack had decided against the biscuits (chocolate chip, still warm from the oven) but only temporarily.

Around him as he ate, above the sound of his munching, was the great clattering din of many children, talking and laughing in the big, echoey room.

Hearing noise, Jack remembered, was a sure sign that you are left out of whatever is happening. He had realised that at Kerry Road. If you're with others, caught up in a game or a talk, you only hear what you're doing. But if you're out of it, you hear other people's conversations, the noise of the whole room, the whole school! And right now,

Jack could hear *everything*.

On the other hand, he didn't mind. He was alone in a little pocket of quiet and he was glad of the rest, glad that he could stop being the New Boy just for a moment. Besides, it meant he could look around. And he saw some interesting things.

The huge dining hall, the diamond patterned windows, the long wooden tables, the plates of cake: all were grander, richer, more colourful versions of things at Kerry Road.

But other things were just plain odd.

The boys, for example. Every one was wearing a different uniform on top. Looking above the tables, he saw blues and greys and blacks and whites; the odd bit of red and dark green; and – for some poor boys dotted here and there – stripes, a straw hat, ties, even bow ties; and, in one case, a long black cloak and top hat (yes, there was Zed, sitting at the next table, crumbling a small bit of cake on his plate and looking totally bored and... what was the word? *aloof*: kind of above everyone and everything around him). All of this looked strange to Jack, like a gathering of different scout groups or – because the boys were tall and short, younger and older, fat and thin, white and brown and black – like representatives from different tribes.

But then, to look under the tables, well, it was just a scrum of muddy knees, torn jeans, odd socks and tatty trainers. Just normal boys, really. Or how normal boys are supposed to be. Jack had never had much chance to get like that, unless he was playing sport.

And another thing caught his attention. Tipping his head right back and looking up at the high beams of the ceiling, Jack could just make out some carving on one of them. It looked like the letters MLB. And then, further along, RJW. Were they initials? It could have been the men that built the roof. He knew that stonemasons used to leave signs on the stones they carved, so maybe roofers did the same? But surely they wouldn't scratch them so roughly, in wonky letters, like with a compass or something?

Jack popped a warm lump of dripping scone into his mouth as he considered. *So if it isn't the roofers, could it possibly be that...?*

"More tea Jack?" Mrs Hopewell was moving along the lines of boys carrying a gigantic teapot and a huge jug of squash, and now she had got to him.

"Yeff Pleafth!" He held out his mug and swallowed heavily, wiping away a few stray crumbs from his face as Mrs Hopewell filled it to the brim with steaming dark tea. Jack helped himself to milk from the jug on the table.

"We always have tea and cake on a Monday," she said, "so that it fits with Mr Bonham's English lesson. And how are you settling in so far Jack?"

"Okay."

"Good. Your stuff's all in your room now, so you can put your duvet cover on and make it feel a bit more like home. And remember, you can come and see me any time if you need to talk about anything. I'm just down the corridor from you."

"Okay. Thank you."

Mrs Hopewell smiled and moved along. Jack had just popped the last bit of jammy, creamy scone into his mouth and was licking his fingers when Mr Bonham stood up and clapped his hands together.

"Okay boys, Okay! If I could just have quiet for a moment please, I have a few things to say."

The talking and clatter quickly died away – so quickly, in fact, that a boy on the other side of the room was left shouting 'CHUCK US A...' and had to end in a whispered *'biscuit!'* as everyone laughed.

"Thank you James," Mr Bonham continued. "Yes do pass him a biscuit someone. Now, where was I? Oh yes, three things I need to tell you." He cleared his throat. "Firstly, everyone, we have a new boy who has joined us today..."

Jack's face immediately went hot and red and he knew that all eyes would soon turn to him.

"Where are you Jack? Ah, there he is! This is Jack everyone and he will be with us for at least a few weeks. So please, do all you can to welcome him and tell him what he needs to know. And Jack, we very much look forward to having you at this school and all the things that you will bring to it."

There were scufflings and scrapings as boys who had not known he was there and could not get a good view moved their chairs and craned their necks to see him. Jack risked looking up and facing the Attention.

His eyes immediately met those of Zed who looked coolly back and raised an eyebrow, as if to say *how very boring this is*. Embarrassed, Jack turned away and saw Wilf, smiling encouragingly from the same table. Several of the other boys, too, were looking at him in a friendly kind of way. He felt better.

"Secondly," Mr Bonham said, to Jack's great relief. "I have had a letter from the National Schools Board. It says that St Cuthbert's may need to have some kind of inspection. I will find out what this is all about, but let's look forward to this great opportunity to show off our wonderful school!"

Strange... thought Jack. At Kerry Road, every inspection was dreaded, a reason for total panic...

"And thirdly, tonight is, of course, our English lesson, so please meet down at the Circle by six o clock..."

The Circle?

"...Kestrel House, I think you are on wood duty..."

Wood duty?

"...so you need to take enough wood from the store to get the fire going..."

Fire going!

"Any questions? Good. Then I will see you all later."

And that was that. Tea mugs were drained, cakes were finished, chairs were scraped back. Everyone seemed to know, in a relaxed yet purposeful kind of way, exactly where they were going.

All apart from Jack. He looked around and, with a little wave of relief, saw Vinnie.

"C-come on Jack. We're going to the c-common rooms 'til six. I'll show you."

And together they walked from the hall.

~ ~ ~ ~ ~

"So, what exactly happens in English then?"

"You'll see. But it's good."

Jack was sitting in an old armchair close to the radiator in one of the common rooms, big old rooms full of sofas and chairs and cushions and lamps and a few tables. Other boys he recognised from the Den were

65

there – Wilf, Angelo and other nameless ones – playing cards, talking, reading. There was no sign of Zed anywhere, much to Jack's relief.

He looked around him. There were lots of cupboards in the room and through their open doors Jack could spot board games, books, comics and annuals. There were even great baskets of Lego and Meccano, lined up against the wall. And now Jack noticed weird and wonderful models made out of both of these, set out on a shelf nearby. There was a brilliant looking rocket launcher; a vehicle with a high crane rising out of it; what looked like a tall ship; and others he couldn't identify from where he was sitting.

"They're the models everyone votes to k-keep," Vinnie said, seeing Jack looking. He himself was draped sideways across an armchair, legs hanging over one side, kicking up and down.

"People think Lego and stuff is for little k-k-kids but it's for all ages. It's scientific to design and build things. Mr Bonham says in Sweden, they get to make stuff all the way through school and that's why that place has good designers. We k-keep the best ones and the rest get broken up. That one..." he pointed to a very intricate model of a tower and wheel with various pulleys, "That's a working mine! This boy Toby built it. He's not here anymore, but I remember him."

Jack stood up and went closer to the shelf. These models were amazing! *How did...? And would it work if...?*

"All right, Jack? I'm your other room mate."

Jack turned to see the boy he had climbed past at the tree house, hands in pockets, grinning broadly at him. He was a big, round-shaped boy in a black sweatshirt that just said DALTON in chunky white letters across the front. He was slouchy and scruffy in a way that made Jack feel at ease; and his face, round and smiling with glasses, exactly matched the drawing on the door.

"Are you Charlie? I saw your drawings. They're really good!"

"Thanks!" Charlie looked pleased. "I'll show you Studio 3 tomorrow if you want? I'm drawing that lot over there right now." He held up a grubby piece of paper and Jack saw a sketch of a few boys playing cards. It didn't look quite right: the table was kind of floating in the air and one of the boys had been rubbed out too many times for you to see him properly. But it was still good.

"It's taking ages," Charlie said. "Anyway, see you later!" And he wandered off to sit at one of the lamp-lit tables.

"You c-can draw in here," Vinnie said. "And do building work. Or you c-can do any quiet stuff, like reading or writing or games. Or talking. But you have to go outside to be loud or mess around. It's quite hard to do homework in here 'c-cos it still gets quite loud..."

There *was* a lot of talking, it was true. Not the echoey chatter of the big hall, more like a warm, loud hum. Like a giant bee.

"Most people go to the library for homework," Vinnie continued. "Or here when it's quiet. Or just do it in their rooms."

"What if you don't do it?" Jack had been worrying about this. "What happens then?"

For the first time, Vinnie looked quite surprised at what Jack was asking.

"That never happens!" he said. "Well, hardly ever. And anyway, we don't get much."

"Oh." Jack pondered this. He could not see why homework would be any less boring here. And with no one to go on at him to get it done, why would he do it, without the threat of some horrible punishment? He was relieved, of course. So many things about St Cuthbert's seemed somehow old fashioned, he would not have been surprised to hear Vinnie say *If you don't do your homework, you get beaten! With a stick!* But then, he couldn't really imagine Mr Bonham, with his fossils, doing that. So why was he magically going to do his homework here?

But it was too much to think about. It was all too different.

"Wanna play C-connect Four Jack?" Vinnie was holding up the box.

~ ~ ~ ~ ~

At a few minutes to six, Jack found himself walking with all the other boys across the grass lawn at the back of the house. Like them, he was wearing his warmest jumper and coat and had a head torch to light the way. *Like coal miners* he thought.

Most of the other boys were talking but Jack was happy to walk along quietly, his hands in his pockets, taking in the strangeness of everything around him. The air smelt clearer than at home and thinner somehow, like he could breathe it in more easily. It smelt of earth and wet trees and faintly of wood smoke.

Together they walked alongside a dark tumble of bushes and flower beds, down some stone steps, past the silver gleam of a large pond and then, ahead of them, Jack saw the dark shadows of trees.

He tilted his head back and looked up at the sky. Stars! Bright stars!... More stars, in fact, the longer he looked. And the moon a yellowy-silver circle with a rubbed out edge. He used to see the moon at home sometimes, when he helped his mum to put out the bins. It would appear briefly over the rooftops. But the stars were always so faint there, he could barely see them. *Because of the street lamps*, his mum said. But here was different! Here was sharp and clear and... *Wow!* There were millions of them!

A feeling of wonder grew in Jack; a feeling he had never had before that filled his whole body. *How far away and endless were the stars... How strange that he, Jack Everett, was alive and here, in this place.*

He walked in under the trees, following the chatting, jostling group. At once he smelt wood smoke stronger than ever, heard the loud cracking of a big fire and saw a bright orange glow ahead. Around it, he could just make out the black silhouettes and here and there the glowing faces of boys – of Kestrel team – tending the fire as they waited.

He hurried forward towards the warmth.

Eight

The roaring bonfire was in a large clearing in the trees, surrounded by a wide circle of log seats and here and there, a few sheets of plastic spread on the ground. Around it, Kestrel boys were throwing on small bits of wood and poking at the blaze with big sticks.

"Hey Ed, no more! I told you, we're letting it go now!" shouted one of the boys.

"All right! It was only a twig – keep your hair on!"

Other boys were already sitting on a few of the stumps, watching.

Mr Bonham was there too at the side of the fire, his face and white hair lit up by the flames. As the others arrived he clapped his hands together loudly.

"Well done Kestrel boys. You've timed it about right I think. Shall we all sit?"

Vinnie grabbed Jack's arm. "C-come on, let's get a stump!"

And suddenly, all the boys were running for the logs, leaving Jack standing alone. There were tussles and raised voices as everyone tried to get a good seat but as the New Boy, Jack did not feel right about joining in. Instead, he perched next to some younger boys on a piece of canvas facing the fire. It was cold to sit on and his back was chilly too, but soon his hands and face were scorched a nice, good hot by the flames. While the others chatted, he sat and stared at the colours and shapes dancing before him and soon he saw that the fire was beginning to burn lower.

Then, off to the side, he noticed another man – *a teacher? The caretaker?* – tending something on a second much smaller fire, which was just a glowing layer of reddish coals. A delicious smell soon began to waft over to Jack and he breathed it in.

Sausages! He's cooking sausages!

"Okay everyone…" Mr Bonham called out eventually. "I want to thank Kestrel boys for getting such a good fire going. It's been a long time now since we had a damp smoking squib for an English lesson, or a blazing inferno that threatens to burn our seats as well! You've all learnt well about keeping wood dry, building up a fire and timing it just right. Thank you too to Mr Kay for doing the sausages."

Mr Kay, bundled in a coat and scarf, his glasses flashing in the firelight, gave a small bow. He looked about Jack's mum's age.

"Joe," said Mr Bonham, "Do you want to hand them out? And Angelo, take round the bread rolls."

A tall boy with brown floppy hair that fell in his eyes went forward and collected a tray of sausages from Mr Kay and a Chinese boy with a shaved head grabbed a big bag of bread rolls. They both started to go round the circle.

"Joe! Angelo! Over here!"

"Joe, you owe me remember!"

"Quick I'm starving!"

And soon everyone including Jack was holding a fat, floury hotdog in their hands. Jack bit into his and was soon munching on the most delicious sausage he had ever eaten: crispy and sticky on the outside and steaming hot in the middle. There was a short lull in the talking and shuffling as everyone concentrated on eating.

"In a while," Mr Bonham announced, swallowing a last mouthful. "I will tell you a story I've wanted to tell you for a while now. But first, a word game!" He wiped his hands on a handkerchief.

"I'm going to give each of you a word and I want you to give me a sentence with that word in. But it's harder than that. Each sentence must follow on from that of the boy before you and together they must make a story. So, listen to what others say, keep an idea of the wider picture and try to lay the ground for people ahead if you can. If you don't understand a word, just say.

Any questions? Yes, Ben? No, there aren't any more sausages. But that reminds me, Mr Kay, do you want to put the next course on?"

Mr Kay took what looked like a bucket of silver and began – to the sound of much cheering – to unload foil-wrapped packages (*what could they be?*) and put them on the glowing coals of the smaller fire.

"Okay," Mr Bonham said, turning to the first boy to his right. "Ben, your word is 'sly'. Begin."

"Um..."

Ben was a brown skinned boy with huge brown eyes that looked almost liquid in the firelight. "I'm not very good at word stuff..."

"It doesn't matter. That's why we're doing this. The best way to learn words, grammar, spelling, punctuation is to read books. Read, read, read as much as you can. But if you're not a great reader – and I know, Ben, that science and experiments are more your Thing – then this game is a good way to learn new words. And remember everyone, by definition, learning something means you didn't know it before, so don't worry about not knowing! That's the point! And together hopefully we will learn some new words. So, Ben, 'sly'..."

"Um yeah. I think it means someone who is... clever, but in a bad way. For bad things?"

"That's right. Sly, cunning, shrewd... all of these words mean that someone is clever, has a sharp brain, but is using their cleverness for certain purposes. If they're sly or cunning, they have a hidden plan, probably to benefit themselves and not entirely fair. We've all heard of the sly old fox that uses his cunning to get the chickens! But if someone is shrewd, then they are clever at judging things and weighing them up to advantage, but not necessarily in a bad way. Being shrewd is pretty useful. So, a sentence with 'sly' in it Ben."

Ben looked more confident. "There was a sly man who lived down the road who was making a clever plan to rob a bank."

"Go Ben!" someone shouted.

"Good. Okay, James, 'suspicious'."

The next boy, one of the few in a bow tie, spoke up immediately. "Many of his neighbours were deeply suspicious of this man."

"Good! Suspicious means you've got ideas that someone is guilty of something. Joe, 'collaborate'."

"I don't know what that means Mr Bonham," Joe said, wiping his hands on his coat.

"Can anyone tell him?"

Lots of hands shot up. To his surprise, Jack noticed that one of them was his.

"Jack?"

Me? He had a moment of panic as everyone looked. But then heard himself say, "I think collaborate means when you work together with someone."

"Good!"

Jack beamed inside.

"So, Joe," Mr Bonham went on. "'Collaborate.'"

"Um... well. The sly man wanted to find someone to collaborate with for his plan?"

"Good. Wilf, 'astronomy'."

"Oh I know!" shouted Ben. "It's stars and stuff!"

"Yes, but don't shout out boys. Give the person whose turn it is a chance to know. Wilf, did you know that astronomy meant the study of matter in outer space?"

"I did actually, so ... The only problem was, the man needed to find someone who knew about astronomy, because the stars were very important to his plan."

The game moved on and Jack went from being nervous to getting caught up in the mad story that was evolving, now involving a Pterodactyl, a murderous baker and all sorts of other twists and turns. When it was his turn, the word was 'dubious'. He knew what it meant straight away.

"The police were dubious about whether the baker's pet kangaroo could really have committed the robbery?"

"Good! Well done. 'Dubious' meaning doubtful, unsure or uncertain. Harry, your word is 'blancmange'."

"What!" protested the boy next to Jack, as everyone laughed. "How do I make a story out of that?"

But Jack was barely listening as the story moved round to the right. He was trying to hide his smile. *Mr Bonham said Good! Well Done!* Instead he watched as Mr Kay put on gardening gloves and began to collect the hot foil parcels from the fire.

Ten minutes later, the game was over and the slightly cooled parcels were being passed around the circle along with spoons. Jack opened his carefully and a puff of hot steam escaped. He looked to Harry next to him.

"Banana and Mars Bar!" Harry said happily, before digging in with his spoon.

Jack looked down. The steam had cleared to reveal a banana with its skin cut open on one side, the hole bursting with an oozing mess of golden brown. He took some on his spoon, blew on it to cool it down and took his first mouthful of hot, fire-baked banana mixed with melted toffee and chocolate.

Wow! He closed his eyes. It was that good.

~ ~ ~ ~ ~

"Tonight," Mr Bonham looked round the circle of fire-lit faces, "the story I want to tell you is actually a real one, about a friend of mine, a very old friend, who has travelled a great deal and seen much of the world. We'll call him John."

The foil and spoons had been cleared away, fingers had been licked or wiped on trousers and most of the boys had shuffled and settled. All were now staring at Mr Bonham who was himself gazing into the fire, his face lit by the now flameless but deeply glowing wood, his hair an orange halo round his head.

"This thing that happened to John occurred when he was still fairly young, at the beginning of his adventures. Which was terrible really because his life could have ended right then, and it so nearly did."

Jack pulled up his hood to keep warm and waited.

"You have to understand," said Mr Bonham, "that John had always been a restless and adventurous kind of person. Always getting into scrapes at school because he had to climb the biggest tree, or jump the widest ditch or find out just what was on the other side of the woods. But each time he fell over, or got lost, or wet, he learnt something. So that by the time he left school as a young man, he was ready to start the biggest adventure of his life, the thing he had always wanted to do: travel the world!

His friends thought he was mad! It wasn't what they wanted to do at all. But he was determined. And he knew how to look after himself in most ways: he could light a fire, cook, do odd jobs for money, get on with most people and read a map.

He also knew the things he couldn't do, the things he would need to be wary of: he had never learnt to swim properly, for example; and he wasn't good at sums, so he would have to be very careful with money.

But on the whole, he felt ready to be independent and eager for an adventure. Which makes it all the more strange really that he should have got into such a sticky situation so early on; a situation that really could have been the end of him... Though looking back on it, there are perhaps many things he could have done differently."

Here Mr Bonham paused in thought and Jack waited eagerly for what he would say next.

"John began his travels in France, as many people do. He caught the boat across the Channel. There was no tunnel underneath the sea in those days, it was still just a mad plan in someone's head, and only the wealthiest people in the world flew anywhere. From there he headed to Paris, the capital city, just a few hours away by train.

Paris is a beautiful city and John wanted to explore it properly. He found a cheap room in a hostel and every day, after fresh bread and jam and a big bowl of hot chocolate, he set out to do just that.

At first he saw the things that everyone wants to see: the Louvre art gallery, the Eiffel Tower, the Avenue des Champs-Elysees... But soon he was exploring a different Paris: the hidden little back streets; the markets where he could buy bread and cheese; the boats on the River Seine that flows through the middle of the city; and – of course – the people. Rich ladies, young students, artists, bakers or businessmen... John loved to watch people and he learnt much this way.

Soon, however, John's money started to run out. He had brought good savings with him and was very careful but everything was so expensive! Then, one day, disastrously, his remaining money was stolen from his room when he left the window open. It wasn't much but it would have kept him going for another few weeks. Now he had nothing, just the money in his pocket. Barely enough for a few last meals.

He decided to leave Paris as soon as possible. He had the address of a family friend, an artist called Louisa, who lived by the sea. Maybe she could help him find work and he could build up his money again? As luck would have it, the hostel chef was driving that way the very next day. All John had to do was pack his possessions – his clothes, a book, a map, a diary... and be ready.

The cook dropped John at a small town ten miles from the sea, late the next afternoon. *Bonne chance!* he called out as he drove away. *Good luck!*

The town was very quiet and John was hungry. He couldn't resist. He went into a Boulangerie – a baker's – and bought himself a big slice of cold French pizza, covered with thick tomato sauce and olives, and a bottle of fizzy orange, and ate and drank in the shade of the trees in the town square. Then, because the sun was shining and because he had just eaten his bus fare, he set off walking, following the signs to the sea.

It wasn't long before John realised he had made a mistake. The day was boiling hot, the road was dusty and dry, his bag felt heavy, the sun was burning his face and he did not have enough to drink; just a bottle of now warm water from the morning. He plodded on, along small roads with high hedges, kept going by the thought of knocking on Louisa's door and – hopefully! – a hot meal, a bath and a soft bed.

As the afternoon became evening and then night started to fall, John realised it was too late to turn up unannounced at Louisa's door on a Saturday night. As he came to the village, he knew he would have to find somewhere outside to sleep and then go to Louisa's in the morning. The night was warm, the stars were coming out and he had camped out many times in his life. He didn't think it would be too disastrous. Besides, he was exhausted after his walk. He knew he would fall asleep instantly. He decided to head for the beach. The soft sand would cushion his body and he would not be in anyone's way.

Some people believe that disasters always come in threes. John had already had two: his money stolen, and arriving so late in the village. He was now about to have another much worse one. All three disasters could have been avoided with more thought, more experience. But really, John was young and on his travels for the first time and this is how we learn.

The beach was quiet in the dark. The moon and stars were silver clear and the sea was far out, shining in the distance. John felt weary, very weary. He looked along the beach and, seeing the shapes of small boats moored high up on the sand, made his way over there in the hope of a sheltered spot.

As he got nearer, he realised it would be much better to sleep inside a boat. The sand was cold now without the sun and some of the smaller boats were not much bigger than a bed. They would be dry and warm and he would be hidden from anyone coming to the beach. The next morning was Sunday so no fishermen would be going out, and he would be gone early before any families came down to the sea.

He picked a small blue boat that looked about the right size, taking out the oars to give him more room. He shoved a dirty canvas sack under one of the seats and then made his bed on the bottom of the boat, using his bag as a pillow. He climbed in, pulled his warm coat around him and lay down. He was asleep within minutes.

Later, drifting up through sleep, John felt a gentle rocking sensation, as if he were in a cradle. There was a thought at the edge of his conscious mind. But he was too tired, sleep was too wonderful, and he let go and fell back down, down into the deepest sleep he had ever had.

Much, much later, John rose up through sleep again. This time he was lying on his side, his coat over his head to keep out the light, and there was that very gentle rocking feeling again. A rocking feeling and the thought – the growing thought – that something was not quite right. Something, in fact, was very wrong. He almost couldn't bear to face it. But he knew, really, deep down, he knew. He just had to turn his head and open his eyes to confirm it: the blue sky, the rising sun and yes, he was going up and down. He was afloat!

John sat up sharply, all senses awake and alarmed now – and then couldn't believe his eyes. This was worse, far worse than he had thought! All around him was water. In every direction water, as far as he could see. Where was the beach? Where was the village? Where even was there any land at all? And how on earth did he get here?

He calmed his racing mind. The boat can't have been attached. The tide must have come in and washed it out to sea. He must have slept through the whole thing. But where was he? And more importantly, how was he going to get back? He remembered with a groan the oars back on the beach.

But worse than that, he felt a growing fear. He couldn't swim! Only a thin sliver of wood separated him from the endless depths of the sea! What if the boat toppled over in a big wave? What if it sprang a leak? John's heart was beating fast now as he examined the boat for cracks, the field of sea for big waves...

And then he realised another terrible thing! No body knew he was there! He had told no one where he was going and no one he was coming! Only the hostel chef knew that he had even been heading for the village – and why would he check up on him? Wait a minute – what about another boat? His eyes scanned the horizon in search of one... but then he remembered. It was Sunday. No fishermen would be going anywhere. He put his head in his hands and felt nothing but the rising, falling swell of the sea and a feeling of total and utter disaster.

Hours later, almost nothing had changed. The boat had drifted. The sun was burning his face. No other vessel had been spotted. John was hungry. Thirsty. And no clearer as to what he could do. He had taken his water bottle from his bag and was rationing his sips – there was very little in there. He had taken one of his shirts and wrapped it round his head and neck to protect himself from sunstroke.

The only other change was that the waves were starting to get a little bigger and this was making him feel very uneasy indeed. Surely his adventure – his life! – wasn't going to end like this, out in this big sea, miles from anywhere?

He couldn't stand the thought that he just had to drift for hours in this boat, waiting for something to happen. Surely he could DO something?

And then John remembered the canvas sack, the one that had been in the bottom of the boat. Maybe that would have something in it? Something that could help him?

He grabbed the edge of it and dragged it out from under the seat: a rough, brown, stained sack with – yes! – definitely things inside. Tentatively, John opened the bag and peered in, his heart thumping. This was his only chance to make things better and get out of this mess!"

Mr Bonham paused. Nothing broke the silence, apart from a spark popping amongst the dying embers. Jack could only just make out the faces round the fire now, so far had it burnt down. He was feeling cold, too. But he desperately wanted to know what John had found and how he had got back.

Because he did get back, *didn't he?* He went on to have other travels and adventures, Mr Bonham had said...

"Well boys," Mr Bonham said, stirring. "The night is late. I am going to tell you the end, but not yet, not yet. What I want you to do, if you will, sometime over the next week, is to write down what you think John found in the bag and what you think the end of that particular adventure was. What mistakes did he make? What could he have done differently? What would *you* do differently? I look forward to reading your ideas."

Nine

Jack was flying forwards and then back, high up on a great swing, so high his feet were in the sky. And below, like tiny toy figures, everyone he knew gazed up at him: Charlie, Vinnie, Zed too; Wilf, Joe and other nameless boys; Mr Bonham and Mr Kay; Max from home; Ellie, his mum and his dad.

His dad??? Dad!! Happiness swung Jack higher and lighter, so high he would fly off…

But then a bird sang loudly and Jack fell instead from a deep, deep sleep. He felt the fading swinging feeling, the dissolving clouds of his dreams and, for a moment, the sharp loss of his dad all over again. He opened his eyes.

There was his old blue duvet cover, his checked pyjama sleeve. And there, on the chest of drawers, the pasta necklace that Ellie had given him. But everything else was new and different. His hair and skin smelt of wood-smoke, his hands were streaked with wood-ash and chocolate, and there were three other boys in the same room as him.

He looked around. Vinnie was lying on his back, snoring gently. Charlie was humped under the duvet, brown hair peeping from the top. And Zed was curled tightly on his side, facing the door. All was quiet in the room and in the great house beyond.

Time to think! Jack turned on his back, stretching out and pushing his feet into the cooler part of the bed and almost immediately his head was full of pictures from the day before. The Eagles' Den, the blazing fire and John drifting all those years ago in a small wooden boat, out to sea. How *on earth* did he get out of that predicament? Jack began to go back carefully over John's story, listing his mistakes, looking for loop holes, starting with error number one – he really should have learnt to swim!

"What are *you* whispering about?" Zed's sharp voice cut into his thoughts, just as he was considering the sack in the boat. Jack looked across at the other boy sitting up in bed, his face pale and pinched.

"Nothing!"

Zed frowned and climbed out of bed, reaching for his clothes. Then he stopped.

"What is *that*?" He pointed contemptuously at the curl of Ellie's necklace, like it was the stupidest thing he had ever seen.

"That!" Jack stared at it. For a moment he wanted to leap out of bed, hide it, throw it away.

"That," he repeated, "is something my little sister made. For me. To bring here."

Zed sneered. "Your little sister! How very *sweet*." He grabbed his towel and left the room, banging the door behind him.

Jack sighed and pulled the covers up to his nose. Why was Zed so horrible to him? "He's all right really," Vinnie said, awake now and bouncing out of bed.

"He doesn't mean it."

Oh really? Jack was pretty sure he did.

"Yeah, you've just got to ignore him!" Charlie added, yawning and sitting up.

A bell chimed loudly above their room. Time to get up. Jack gave Charlie and Vinnie a small smile.

"I'll try."

What else could he do? There wasn't really anything to tell anyone and he didn't want to be mean back. So ignoring it was the only option. And anyway, he was getting on okay with everyone else. Why should he let Zed ruin everything?

By the time the sounds of morning were well and truly on their way in bumps and scrapes and shouts from other rooms and the boys were all dressed and washed, Jack was ready for the day ahead. And he knew *exactly* what he thought was in the canvas sack at the bottom of the boat. He even had an idea for the roof of the Eagles' Den! He would tell Charlie and Vinnie later.

But he wouldn't tell Zed. Not after the necklace thing. He had a feeling he was going to have to be careful what he said around Zed.

~ ~ ~ ~ ~

At nine o' clock, Jack was sitting in his first lesson of the day. He was full of breakfast (sweet bacon, fried egg, four pieces of toast and jam, orange juice and a cup of hot tea) and he was ready. Mr Kay – his teacher! – was standing in front of the class, adjusting his glasses, a huge pile of books and scrolls and folded papers on the table next to him.

"Good morning everyone. Welcome Jack."

Jack reddened and looked down at the desk he was sharing with Charlie, grateful that he was there. Vinnie and Angelo were sitting a few desks behind. Zed was at the back. Jack recognised most of the other faces from around the fire.

"Today," Mr Kay continued, "we're going to start a new topic, which is good timing for you Jack. We're going to be learning about maps and mapping, a subject which I absolutely love!" He took off his glasses and put them on again, placing his hand on the pile of books which Jack saw now were atlases and folded maps, some new and some looking very old.

"But before we do anything else, I want you all to go off and make your own map of St Cuthbert's."

"Yesss!" hissed voices around the room.

Cool! thought Jack. But he noticed Charlie shifting impatiently in his chair.

"You can work collaboratively in pairs," Mr Kay continued, "but please don't go and find a map of St Cuthbert's to copy because what I'm really interested in is your own impressions. Yes Joe?" The boy with the floppy hair who had handed out sausages the night before had his hand up.

"How much detail do you want Mr Kay? Do we have to put like flower beds and stuff on it?"

"It's entirely up to you. There are no right or wrong maps at this stage. I'm interested in what you think should go on. Yes Charlie? What is it?"

"Mr Kay it's raining. Shouldn't we do this inside?"

Everyone looked to the windows where the wind was indeed blowing light splatters of raindrops against the glass. Mr Kay peered up at the sky.

"I think you might be right Charlie... It looks like it's going to get worse."

There were groans.

"Normally," Mr Kay turned to Jack, "we do part of our lessons outside whether there's rain, wind, sun or snow. *'There's no bad weather, only the wrong clothes and the wrong equipment'* is one of our mottos here and I'm sure you'll find it's true. But today, I want you to be able to discuss and draw properly, so you'll need to be dry. And you all know the grounds well enough by now. So, take some of the big sheets of paper on the side there, and go and find somewhere quiet – the library, the common rooms, the hall – and get started. I'll be here if you need to come and ask anything."

There was a loud scraping sound as boys moved back their chairs, took their things and then noisily made their way out of the room. Only Charlie remained and Jack, who was waiting for him.

"Mr Kay..." said Charlie, a bit pleadingly. "Jack doesn't know the grounds yet. Can I like give him a quick tour? So he knows what's here?"

Mr Kay regarded them both. "Well, you do need to see it all Jack, or none of this will make sense. Though I'm not sure why you're so keen Charlie!" He narrowed his eyes. "But as long as you do a quick tour and then catch up on your map making later, that's fine."

"Yess! Thanks Mr Kay!" Charlie turned and smiled. "Come on Jack. Let's get kitted out."

As they left the room, Charlie pulled something from his pocket and showed it to Jack, something red. It was the end of a scarlet strip of material.

They were going to tag a Den!

~ ~ ~ ~ ~

"What did you say?!"

The rain was rattling like small stones on the hood of his waterproof and Jack could hardly hear Charlie's voice. Boys from a younger class, in various uniforms, were taking it in turns to run from the main building to the much smaller one opposite. Jack could just make out the sign stuck to the window: **Studio 3**

"I said," Charlie shouted at Jack, gesturing to a big barn-like building opposite Studio 3. "Shall we go in there a minute? Just 'til everyone's gone? We don't want them to see us heading for the woods!" Droplets were pouring down his face and running across his glasses, like rain on a window.

He needs mini windscreen wipers thought Jack. *Or awnings, like shops have. They could pop out when it rains! Striped. No, black. That would be cool!"*

Charlie pushed open the big door and Jack followed inside to a gloomy and suddenly silent, thick-walled room.

"Phew! That's better!" Charlie pulled down his hood, took off his glasses and began to clean them on his glove. "Welcome to the junk room! I think the light's bust."

Jack looked around and saw that the room was indeed full of junk: old prams, a washing machine, bits of wood of all sizes, some plant pots, black bin bags full of soft stuff – clothes? – and cardboard boxes full of smaller items. He could just see, poking out, some old fairy lights, a piece of rope and a teapot. In a pile nearby were about ten broken and twisted umbrellas.

"This is where we store all the useful stuff that the school doesn't need anymore, or that we get from the tip."

Jack gazed round and his eyes started to pick out other items: a shop's dummy, a basketball hoop, a great pile of newspapers, about two hundred empty, flattened cereal boxes...

"Useful for what?"

"Oh, everything really," Charlie said airily, peering out of the milky, cobwebbed window next to the door. "Junk modelling, art projects, Design and Technology challenges – you know. This year it's making dens but last year it was *Make an Outdoor Kitchen*. We made a BBQ out of a shopping trolley and sharpened tons of knives out of sticks."

"Did you...we... win?"

"Nah, Kestrels did. They collected all these outdoor plants to use. Wild garlic, elderflowers, stuff like that."

Jack spotted a collection of old wheels lying on the floor, arranged in size: tiny chunky ones, thin racing ones and huge wagon-like wheels.

"Do people bring their bikes here?"

"Yeah, some do. But we mostly use stuff that's already here. Over there look."

Jack peered through the gloom and spotted a sideways pile of rather old looking bikes leaning against a wall and some scooters scattered on the floor around them.

"We ride them at this place called The Paths, at the bottom of the field..."

Did this mean he would finally get to ride a bike without an adult around?

"...Look, I'll draw a quick plan while we wait. We can use it later."

The greyish light flashed on Charlie's glasses as he rummaged in his pocket and took out some folded paper and a pen and started sketching. He drew a big square building in the middle of the page, two smaller squares next to it – Studio 3 and the Junk Shed? – and then paths and squares of land.

"Were you always good at drawing?" Jack asked. "Or did you learn it here?"

"Well…" Charlie paused. "I liked art at Dalton. That was my old school."

"I worked that out!"

"Oh yeah – the sweatshirt. Subtle isn't it!" He laughed and then carried on sketching. "The thing is, we never did much art. And I was rubbish at everything else. I always came last in tests and they said I caused loads of trouble 'cos I messed about. They didn't like me. They even tried to get me out of school once, so I wouldn't be there for an inspection and spoil it for them!"

Charlie pressed hard on his pencil and drew a sharp black line at the bottom of the page, almost tearing the paper.

"Can they do that?"

"Well, they did. My mum went mad. But then this artist guy came to the school for a bit, to do art with us. Quite an old guy. Mr Lucas his name was. And he let us work on anything we wanted. It was brilliant! I got really into Leonardo da Vinci – do you know him?"

Jack shook his head.

"He's this artist and he's *amazing*. He lived, like, hundreds of years ago but he was good at everything – drawing, music, maths, everything! He did brilliant drawings of people and he designed loads of cool inventions, like flying machines and stuff. It made me want to learn more about him and draw more. So when

Mr Lucas left, he suggested me for St Cuthbert's. That was last year and here I am!"

"Bit like what happened to me with Rupert Woolacroft," Jack said thoughtfully. "I guess Mr Lucas must be on the Board too."

Charlie shrugged and peered out of the window again.

"Hey, they've all gone! Come on! We'll go round the building first and then down to the woods. There's only me and you left to find the Dens, everyone else in Eagles has done it. And you're new, so it's fair to go together."

Jack followed Charlie out of the door and into the rain, pulling his hood up as he went.

"Studio 3!" Charlie called as they passed it. "I'm there all the time. That's why I haven't found any Dens yet."

As they got to the end of the building, Jack saw the field that led to the Eagles' Den. But instead they followed the wall of the school and soon came round to the front where the driveway, white and straight, stretched away through meadows to the world outside. As they passed the stone steps leading to the main door and Mr Bonham's long study windows (was it really just *yesterday* that he had arrived?) Jack glanced inside and saw a most unusual sight. The Headmaster was standing in the middle of the room, swinging his arms in a massive movement and then leaping up and down. Jack couldn't hear anything, but it looked like he was cheering. *What the...?*

"Practising his cricket swing," Charlie said. "He's just scored a six."

They carried on past.

"How come Vinnie's here?" Jack asked, thinking of cricket.

"Vinnie? He was hyper active at school or something like that. Always fidgeting and not listening and distracting everyone. His mum took him to the Doctor's to get this medicine that makes you calm, but the Doctor wouldn't give it to him. She had other ideas. Turns out her dad used to go here a long time ago or something and he recommended Vinnie."

"And Wilf?" asked Jack. "Why didn't he like school? He seems the sort of boy who would."

"Wilf's really dyslexic. You know, that thing where you can't read or write letters well? And he was at one of those proper posh schools, really competitive he said. They did help him but they still made him feel stupid he says. His dad knew someone who had been here, so..." Charlie shrugged.

"And Zed?" Jack asked. "How did he get here?"

The two boys turned the corner of the building and were now approaching the kitchens. Metal clanging sounds danced out into the morning rain along with the buttery smell of frying onions.

"Oh, Zed!" Charlie gave a little smile. "He's been here ages. His story's a bit different..."

But at that moment, a round woman in a blue checked apron appeared at a side door, shaking out a tablecloth.

"Hello Mrs Walker! What's for lunch?" Charlie asked hungrily.

"Shepherd's Pie." She smiled. "And Treacle Pudding."

"Yesss!" Charlie and Jack looked happily at each other. They were already hungry. But they left the buttery onion smell behind them and crunched along the gravel until they were once again at the back of the building, facing Studio 3 and the Junk room. In between, a white path led away from the school to the rest of the grounds and the distant, thicker woods.

"Right," said Charlie. "No one's about. Let's go and find a Den!"

Jack's heart leapt. And without a word, the two boys set off at a run.

Ten

Jack's breath panted and echoed round his waterproof hood as he ran at full tilt in the rain alongside Charlie.

"Vegetables!" Charlie shouted, as they ran past some gardens and Jack saw raised beds, cabbages and rows of other green things at different stages of growth or decay.

Next came a normal garden, with trellises and flower-beds, benches and rose bushes, all green now but here and there a few purple flower heads clung on in the rain.

After that came stone steps set in a gentle grass bank. The boys clattered down and passed the pond from the night before, now a great brown circle, dimpled with rain.

And now playing fields. Rugby and football goals, an over-grown cricket pitch and over to the right, a rough-looking tennis court. Beyond all that, a shaky view of trees and denser woods.

Wow! Amazing!

Jack felt a soaring sense of freedom suddenly, almost as though he could fly. He was boiling too. He pulled off his hood and ran faster and Charlie did the same. Delicious cool rain fell onto their faces and their heads and they laughed. Jack didn't know why! It just felt so good!

"You're fast man!" Charlie shouted, panting. Jack grinned. He loved running!

"There!" gasped Charlie suddenly, as they came to the first trees and slowed down. "The Paths!"

Through the lighter woods to the right, still quite far away, the ground rose to a high bank, almost a hill really, that bordered the school grounds in that direction. And down the side of the hill, in various wiggly lines, snaked long and curving paths. Some of them were really steep looking and just calling out for a scooter – or a bike! The main path was huge, long and almost vertical. Surely no one rode down that. *Did they?*

"There are mud bumps over there too, in the trees. We have to keep doing them 'cos the rain washes them away."

"Can we...?"

"No we better get back by morning break, or Mr Kay won't let me do this next time. We go that way..." He pointed to the left where the woods became much thicker. "That's the only bit where there could be a Den. So hopefully we'll find one on the way back." He stopped suddenly, struck by a thought, and rummaged in his pockets to pull out some very sticky looking boiled sweets. "Want one?"

Jack took a tacky red lump and started to pick off the plastic wrapper that was melded to the sweet. The cherry taste, when he got to it, was delicious.

"Come on!" said Charlie, thickly, through his sweet. And they set off deeper into the woods.

The boys walked companionably and in silence, apart from the odd sucking sound and the mulch of their boots on the wet ground. Thick lines of trunks were gnarled and smooth, silvery and dark. Branches and fallen trees were brown and slippy. Many leaves – yellow, amber, bronze, brown – were clumped and wet underfoot, and there was a steady pattering of rain from above. Here and there, clumps of evergreen trees made up darker patches in the woods. And for the first time, Jack felt he was really *in* autumn. Not watching it on television or doing an organised trail through the park. Just... in it.

"What exactly are we looking for?" he asked Charlie eventually, his eyes scanning the trees before him.

"Dunno! Anything!" Charlie grabbed a long stick and started bashing some of the bushes, as if something might be hiding in the middle of them. "Any sign that the others have been here, or that there might be a camp." He stopped bashing for a moment and turned to Jack.

"Our Den's obvious 'cos we wanted the biggest tree and the swing and it's so near school. Everyone tagged it in like a day! But the other Dens are more secret. It's taken people ages to find them anyway. Wilf said look in the thickest part. There are no really big trees here, so it's got to be really hidden, or clever..."

Jack nodded and the two boys continued through the woods, picking through falling branches and surveying all they passed. Jack's eyes raked the leaves and twigs and trees for any sign of habitation or disturbance. But nothing. And nothing for quite some time... And then suddenly:

"Hey! Look here!" Charlie was bending over to pick up something from the ground. Jack ran over.

"What is it?"

Charlie held up a small, round, yellow pin badge in his fingers. "It's a Falcon badge. I bet they have a Den near here. Let's search round a bit."

Jack and Charlie moved away from each other, peering up at tree tops, through bushes and down at the ground, looking for further signs. But it was Jack who made the discovery. Behind lots of bushes, he spotted the top of a strange Weeping Willow shaped tree where all the branches hung down, creating a curtain of green, like a big marquee. He made his way over and tentatively parted the leaves.

"Charlie!" he shouted. "Quick!"

Charlie came crashing through the undergrowth and followed Jack inside the curtain. "Wow!"

The two boys looked around in wonder. They were in a cave, a dark green cave, made of leaves. The central trunk of the tree stretched up before them, straight and strong, and the roof arched above them and then trailed back to the ground. Amazingly, the tree cave was completely dry. Not a single drop of rain had come through. And there were smaller caves too, where branches hung down and partitioned off parts of the space, like rooms. And inside the dry rooms, boys had left some of their possessions: an old blanket, a tracksuit top, a book. There were a few small platforms too where branches joined the trunk, just big enough for storing things: some half eaten packets of biscuits, closed up with a twist; a few comics; and things the boys must have found in the wood: weird shaped fir cones, huge bright yellow leaves and various twisted sticks.

"I like it..." said Charlie softly, looking around. "I never even knew this tree was here."

Jack loved it. It was so secret and hidden and cosy almost.

"Is it Falcon's?" he asked.

"Definitely. Partly 'cos of the badge. But mainly 'cos that's Sam H's school tie over there, tied to that branch." Jack saw a green and gold striped tie, dangling from the tree.

They surveyed the cave quietly, respectfully considering the artistry of the Den.

"It's good," said Charlie, eventually. "But ours is better."

Jack had to agree, it was. And, even though he had not built any of it himself, he felt the first feelings of pride that he was an Eagle.

"Look!" said Charlie, pointing to a smaller branch. It was covered in red and blue strips of material where others had tagged the Den in the same place. "Come on, let's get ours up somewhere different. And we'd better get a move on if we want to get back in time."

He pulled the red tie from his pocket and looked around. "There?"

Jack looked up to where he was pointing and saw the main horizontal branch in the cave, the one you would see as soon as you came in, and he nodded.

Charlie clamped the red tie between his teeth and started to climb the main trunk, using the forks of smaller branches to reach it. Once there, he shuffled out along the branch and fastened the tie.

It hung – a thin, bright red flag – glowing slightly in the cave. A sign that the final two Eagles had been there.

~ ~ ~ ~ ~

"What would you like to work on Jack?"

Trudy, the artist who helped to run Studio 3, had come over to talk to him. Outside, the rain had cleared and a gold, autumn sun was shining through the skylight in the roof. What was it his Grandma used to say? *If there's enough blue sky to make a man a shirt, it's going to be a nice day.* His dad had always liked that.

"Jack?"

Trudy was still looking at him, her hands in the pockets of her overalls and a questioning look on her face. She had a nice face, with freckles and red hair like his. Though he didn't have plaits, obviously.

"Um...I'll do the self portrait one, the thing you said it's good to start off with."

"Okay, that's good. It'll be interesting. Just help yourself to anything you need."

She indicated the paints and papers, glues and brushes, pallets and other art and craft materials that lined the walls on shelves and in boxes. "And you know the rules now, don't you."

He did. And they were pretty good. In fact, he couldn't have invented better ones himself. The studio belonged to the children. Every year, they voted for a Management Team and that team then ran the studio, made up the rules, ordered the paints, kept the room tidy and raised money for materials, mainly through running a shop. But as Tom, the Treasurer, had told him, *any enterprising idea will be considered.* A hand drawn poster on the wall near the door set out the most recent rules and they were quite simple:

1. Respect other people's work
2. Don't waste paint!
3. Clear up after yourself
Signed: The Management

Apart from that, you could do pretty much any project or idea you wanted to in Studio 3!

Right now, some boys were working on the floor, painting or drawing on big sheets of paper. Angelo was making a volcano out of paper mache. Another boy was using a projector to shine an enlarged copy of his drawing of a dinosaur onto the wall and was drawing round the huge outline. And Joe had attached huge sheets of paper to the wall near Jack and was flicking paint against it with his brush. Great splats of blue, yellow and red arced across the paper in a random yet strangely satisfying pattern. As Jack looked, quick-fire black splatters landed on the floor near his feet, a couple of them hitting Trudy's shoes as she passed.

"Oops, sorry!" said Joe, pausing.

"No worries," said Jack, moving back slightly. Trudy didn't bat an eyelid. The concrete floor was anyway covered with a million spots of paint and glue.

"It's what it's for," she said, catching Jack's eye. "You can't have an artists' studio where you can't get messy!"

And she went to get on with her own work.

Jack looked round again at what others were doing. In one corner, a couple of boys were lying on the floor looking at art books and another was writing in a small notebook. In the other corner, Charlie, Zed and a few others were discussing a Comic Club they were setting up. They were going to make a comic and sell it for 50p, Charlie said, to raise money for the studio. And they were working on their invented super-hero right now. Jack gazed longingly over at the group. He had such great ideas for a super hero...

At that moment, Zed looked over and coldly raised an eyebrow. *And?* he seemed to be asking. *What's this got to do with you?*

Jack sighed and turned back to his self-portrait notes. *A good starting point* Trudy had said *is to write or draw the words and things and likes and dislikes that make you You, that make you Jack.* He frowned, chewed his pencil and started to write.

Ten minutes later, the studio door banged open and Wilf came in.

"All right Jack? Where's Trudy? I've got a message for her."

"She's on the roof, setting up her project."

Trudy wanted to take photographs of the studio through the skylight to go with the photographs she had taken of the sky from the studio, and she was trying to find the best spot.

"Well done for tagging the Falcon Den by the way," Wilf said. "We've all done that one now."

"Well, it was Charlie really..." Jack replied modestly.

"Funny – he said that about you. Anyway, you just need to find Kestrel's now."

"By the way, Wilf," Jack decided to seize his moment. "Do you think we could get an old tent from somewhere for the Eagles' roof? One of those big square ones? I thought maybe at the tip..."

"Yes, good idea... There might even be one in the junk room somewhere. I'll ask Alex later."

Jack felt a little glow. *Good idea!* He resolved to think of more good ideas for his team whenever he could. Sucking his pencil, he went back to his list, which was proving quite difficult because things had changed quite a bit over the past two days. So far it read:

Jack Elliott - Self Portrait
Dislikes:
School
Lessons
Soup

Likes:
Food
Family
Scooter
Bikes

Underneath he had added:

Climbing
Running
Stars
Fires
Stories

And, after some thought:

Having Ideas

"Guys, can I just have everyone's attention for a minute!" Trudy, holding her camera, was standing by the door with Wilf. "I've got a note from Mr Bonham here and he wants to let everyone know that the school inspection will be next Wednesday, just over a week away. We've never had one of these before so it's a good chance to show visitors the studio, our artworks and all our enterprise schemes. I'm sure the Management Team will meet about this before then, but does anyone from the Team want to say anything now?"

Tom stepped forward.

"If any paints or materials need ordering before then, let me know. Also, there's a good chance our comics will be ready, so maybe we can sell a few?"

There was a murmur of excitement as the room considered this and then Tom sat back down.

As Wilf left and noise and work resumed, a splatter of gold paint flew through the air and streaked down Trudy's overalls.

"Sorry!" said Joe.

Was Jack the only one who had a bad feeling about inspections? Somehow, he just couldn't imagine one at St Cuthbert's.

Eleven

Dear Mum

Thanks for the new pencils you sent me with your letter and the sharpener that you can screw to a desktop. It's of very high quality. Actually, I can buy pencils from the Studio 3 shop now so don't worry about any replacements. I am well fixed up on the pencil front. And yes, I have used the ink pen! We only use it to do special writing. It makes you write very neatly and carefully.

Sorry I have not written before. Week One has been very busy! You know the map making I told you about on the phone? It turned out that even though there is only one St Cuthbert's, all our maps were different. Angelo didn't even mark the sports pitches on his, because he doesn't play sport. And we all made the school way too big. Now we're learning all about standards when you make a map, so that everyone in the world can understand them, and also about scale, so like where every 10 metres in real life might be One cm on the map.

Did you know, the Australian Aborigines used to make maps out of stories and art? Charlie would have made a good aborigine. Charlie's the boy I told you about here that I get on well with, and Vinnie, and Wilf and all the others. Well, nearly all the others.

We've started our autumn study where every week we're recording stuff that changes. I've collected loads of conkers off the trees and we've been playing that game Dad told me about, when he was little? My best conker is a 5-er, but I've only been here a week. This boy called Jack B in Kestrel has a 52er, but Mrs Walker baked it in the school oven for him. It might be cheating. We're trying to decide. Remember you said Dad once had a 92er?! I can but dream.

Good news! I got my first bit of written homework back for English and it said Very Good Creative Thinking and Problem Solving!

You said do we get free time and yes we get loads. We mainly work outside on our Design and Technology challenge. I'm sorry but I can't tell you any more about that because you are not in Eagles. If I tell you, I will have to kill you. Ha ha!

Just joking, but it is Top Secret. I will just say I go in the woods a lot!

Studio 3 is cool too. I've joined Comic Club and we're working on a story about Bird Man, a super hero who can turn himself into any bird and who can call all the birds of the world to help him. Would you or Ellie like to order one? It's a bargain! Only 50p. What about Mrs Watson next door?

Anyway, I better go. It's tea in a minute - cottage pie and then cornflake treacle tart and custard, the menu board says. But of course I do miss your cooking too.

Please will you give these letters to Ellie and Max? Also one for Rupert Woolacroft like you asked me to.

Love
Jack XXX

Dear Ellie

Mum will read this to you. Thanks for your picture of Zombie and for the lolly. Would you and your friends like to read all about the Adventures of Bird Man?? Ask Mum to get you the comic!! I will see you when you come and get me at the end of term.

Jack

Dear Max

Thanks for the space poster from by your bed. Good idea to leave the blue tack on. I put it straight up. My corner looks better now. I am hoping to cover more of the white space soon.

To finish what I was telling you on the phone about the John story, I decided this:

- A bottle of water (for hydration purposes)
- Some bars of chocolate (chocolate is high energy!)
- A flare (to alert other ships)
- A bright coloured flag (to alert ships if no one saw the flare)
- Some fishing lines and hooks to catch mackerel (I saw a man do it on telly. But I guess John would have to get pretty hungry to eat raw fish. Though Japanese people do).
- And finally, a blow up life-ring, so no matter what, he wouldn't drown.

There were no rules to say it was not a very big sack.

What Mr Bonham told us really happened was John found water and old hard bread to keep him going, a bell to alert boats, some binoculars, and a life-ring (I was close!). He spotted the coast through the binoculars and started to paddle with his hands in the right direction. He spent the night making sure he didn't drift further away. Then very early, like two in the morning or something, some fishing boats came out and found him. What happened to him after that is another story altogether Mr Bonham says. I wrote all the things he did wrong and I'm pretty sure I wont do any of that when I'm older. I won't ever be stuck on a boat without oars anyway.

I asked Mum on the phone about St Cuthbert's but you can only go if you hate school and are recommended by the board. Sorry for that. It's a shame because you know how you like insects and you're always finding them in cracks in the pavement? Well there's a boy like that here too! He's called Harry and he's a Falcon. He finds LOADS of cool stuff all the time. He showed me a bird's skull he's got.

But see you when I come back and I will tell you everything. Even Eagles stuff!
Jack

PS Would you like to buy a copy of our Bird Man Comic? It's really worth the 50p. Ask people at school! There may be a small addition for postage.

PPS Look up Leonardo da Vinci's flying machine inventions! Charlie let me look at his book about them. They're cool!
Wish I could fly.

Dear Mr Woolacroft

Thank you for recommending me to come here. I am having a great time at St Cuthbert's. I see now why they call it The Wild School! We are outdoors nearly all of the time.

I hope that Café Amazon is progressing well. Do you sell many acky juices?

I wonder how your clients are enjoying your pictures? I found them very interesting. I like weapon design.

Yours gratefully
Jack Elliott.

Dear Dad

I dreamt I saw you again last night. You were in the distance but we never caught up with each other.

I used your penknife yesterday! We had a woodwork lesson with Alex who is the caretaker but he also does gardening and woodwork and stuff. He showed me how to hold it and how to only ever cut away from your body. We had to find a stick in the woods and then carve our own marks on it. Mine was like this:

IIII >>>>> <<<<< IIIII ===== IIIII <><><>

But not as neat.

I like it here Dad and I think you would too. We've done loads at the Den. We've got a roof now which I invented.

And we dragged an old mattress out of the junk room to put under the swing. Now you can go on really, really high and jump off, but I haven't dared do it yet.

Me and Charlie found the Falcon Den in the end too. You wont believe it! It was in an old wooden shed at the back of the tennis courts, like a summerhouse thing. So not even one they made! But I have to admit it was cool inside. They got loads of old paint pots off Alex and Studio 3 and decorated it with all mad pictures. And it's got Harry's nature collection in it, all skeletons and hollow eggs and other cool stuff.

Zed is still mean. He calls me a Mummy's Boy. It started because I got some cake in the post. It wasn't that nice anyway and I couldn't eat it, but Zed saw the note with it and laughed. He thinks it's weak or something to hear from your family. He never ever rings his. It would be bad if he found this letter.

Anyway, I'd better go. Me and Charlie and Vinnie are playing cards tonight for sweets!

Did I tell you there are some old bikes here?

I know I can't send this to you. But if what people tell me is true, you will know it all anyway.

Jack

Twelve

"Charlie! Vinnie! Wake up! We've got to get down to breakfast early remember! It's Inspection Day!" Jack was shaking Charlie's shoulder.

"Humph…" Charlie mumbled. "…Minute."

Jack sighed and sat back on the bed to find Zed eyeing him coolly from the doorway.

"What a good boy you are!" he said scornfully. "Why on earth do you keep going on about this inspection? No one else could care less."

Jack felt a prickle of irritation alongside his usual upset feeling.

"Did you actually have inspections at your old school?" he asked, eyeing the top hat already perched on Zed's head and the cape draped over his arm.

"No, we didn't. And I find the whole thing utterly boring."

He turned and left the room, leaving Jack staring at the pale gold sun streaming through the gap in the curtains.

At breakfast, Jack poured golden syrup patterns all over his porridge and sipped at his mug of tea, but neither tasted as good as usual.

"Cheer up Jack!" Vinnie scraped back a chair and plonked himself next to Jack, grabbing the golden syrup bottle.

"Yeah, what's up?" Charlie sat down on the other side of the table.

"I dunno. I think it's this inspection." He didn't want to mention that it was also Zed, that this boy was really starting to get to him. "I remember them from my old school."

"Well," Charlie pointed with his spoon at the Headmaster who was sitting at a nearby table. "*He* doesn't seem too worried by it."

It was true. Mr Bonham was in fine spirits, humming to himself as he buttered his toast.

"That's what worries me," said Jack. "The fact that it doesn't worry him. My old school would have been in panic mode by now."

"Yeah, Dalton would too," said Charlie thoughtfully. "They would have got rid of me anyway. But St Cuthbert's is different, isn't it?"

At that moment, Mr Bonham brushed the crumbs from his hands and stood up, clapping to get the attention of the hall.

"Okay boys. Just to remind you that today is the day of our inspection visit and I hope you will help show off St Cuthbert's to its very best!" He smiled happily. "Mrs Sharp will be arriving soon and I need two helpful volunteers to show her round…. Giles and Connor, are your hands up? Okay, good. Meet me in the entrance hall at nine thirty and let your teachers know."

Jack looked at Giles and Connor, two Kestrel boys from another class, as they stood up from the next table.

He tried to see them an Inspector might. Was Mr Bonham *mad*? Giles was big and scruffy looking, a tattered old straw hat perched on his head (a *boater* Jack thought they were called) and a pinstriped green and yellow blazer that had seen better days. His hair was long and curly and his trousers were torn.

Connor on the other hand was small and neat... up to a point! His uniform was grey and fairly normal, but it must have been full of holes at some stage because he appeared to have darned them all himself – probably in sewing class – with bright red wool! All over his clothes, there were great crosses and tangles of red, and long stray threads dangling down. Fair enough, he'd done it himself and that was quite an achievement, but he looked odd, to say the least.

And what was that on his feet? Trainers *with the toes cut out? What the...!*

This was going to be a disaster.

"Everyone else," Mr Bonham continued, "Have a great day and I will see you at our English lesson tonight. If our guest stays that long, we can entertain her with a good story around the fire! There's one I've been meaning to tell for a while now."

And he sat down to breakfast, humming again.

Jack pushed his porridge away. He just didn't feel hungry.

"Can I have your toast then?" Charlie looked hopeful.

"Yes, have it!" Jack pushed the plate towards Charlie and then turned to him a bit impatiently. "But Charlie, you've got to admit, this inspection can't go well."

"Inthspxio?" Charlie said, through a buttery mouthful, and then swallowed. "Stop worrying Jack! I've told

113

ST CUTHBERT'S WILD SCHOOL FOR BOYS

you. St Cuthbert's does everything its own way. Why should this be different?"

"Because they're inspectors!"

"So what!" Charlie took another big bite of toast.

"Yes why does it matter?" Vinnie added. "What c-can they do?"

"*What can they do?!*" Jack put down his mug. "They can do anything! They can ban stuff. They can make more rules. I know, 'cos they did that at my school and we couldn't even run in the playground in the end! They could even close the school down you know..."

Charlie frowned for a moment, considering, but then his face cleared.

"Yeah but what if this is a St Cuthbert's type inspector? Mr Bonham wouldn't get just anyone to come here, would he! He'd get someone special."

Jack considered this for a moment. Was it possible? After all his experience at Kerry Road, he doubted it. And yet, so much at St Cuthbert's had surprised him, maybe Charlie was right and this would be the same? A *Wild* inspector coming to visit?

"I suppose. Okay, you're right."

"Good, now pass me the jam."

~ ~ ~ ~ ~

"...Nineteen, twenty, twenty-one..." Jack counted his steps as he ran through the school, rushing to fetch a forgotten pencil case from his room. He always counted his steps when he was on his own.

But as he skidded into the main entrance hall he stopped. Someone was there. Someone who could only be Mrs Sharp. He saw spiky black shoes, a navy blue suit, a raincoat over one arm, a briefcase on the other and hair pulled back into a tight, tight bun. Her mouth was a straight line of bright red lipstick and she was brushing a tiny speck of dust from her jacket. She looked up. "Good morning young man!"

Her voice was sharp like her name and very precise.

"Er... good morning." Jack saw her gaze fall upon his muddy knees, gained in a quick game of football before breakfast.

"Just off to change!" he explained brightly, before dashing upstairs out of sight.

On the way back, in clean trousers, he was just in time to see Mr Bonham introducing Giles and Connor, who were enthusiastically holding out their hands to shake.

"These are the two boys who will be showing you round," Mr Bonham said. "I do think it's best you get the children's view first. They're the important ones after all."

Mrs Sharp was staring in a frozen kind of way at the boys as they stood scruffily and slightly awkwardly now before her.

"Off you go now boys!" Mr Bonham continued happily. "I'll be in here with Zoe when you've finished."

"Zoe?" Mrs Sharp dragged her eyes from Giles and Connor and looked questioningly at Mr Bonham. "I thought this was a boys' school?"

"Oh it is, it is. Zoe's not a person! Zoe is a dog!"

At that mention, Zoe herself came rat tatting to the door. She looked questioningly up at Mrs Sharp, dismissed her, and rat tatted back to the study.

"You keep *a dog* in the school?" Mrs Sharp inquired, rather incredulously.

"Goodness, no. Just Zoe! You can meet her later. And don't worry – we have cats too, if you're more of a cat person."

This was news to Jack but now that he thought about it, there *were* lots of little dishes lying around outside... Excellent! He could continue his Cat Intelligence Experiments from home. But by the look on Mrs Sharp's face, she did not share his enthusiasm.

"Off you all go!" Mr Bonham said, giving a cheerful little wave. "And have fun! I'll see you back here later."

And with that he disappeared into his study, still humming.

Have fun! *Have fun!* Was he mad? Couldn't he see that this person had probably never had fun in her life? And she certainly wasn't going to start here.

As Mrs Sharp began to question the two boys, Jack hurried down the stairs and headed off to his class. But not before he heard the clear, bell-like tones of Giles as he said "Oh no, we don't have assemblies! Just kind of meetings round the fire at night."

Jack rushed through the doors before he could hear her reply.

~ ~ ~ ~ ~

"Never Eat Shredded Wheat!"

Mr Kay pointed at the four points of the compass on the board. "North, east, south and west. But you might want to make up your own way of remembering them. As long as you know the four points, you'll get all the in-betweens like north east, or south west. But let's get outside and do some orienteering and we can come back to the diagram later."

He was just explaining the orienteering task when there was a loud knock at the door. Giles and Connor shuffled in followed by a cold-eyed Mrs Sharp.

"We've brought the visitor," they mumbled, looking even less confident now.

"Mrs Sharp!" Mr Kay held out his hand and she took it, limply. "I'm Mr Kay. We're in the middle of our map project."

Jack followed Mrs Sharp's eyes around the room as she took in the hundreds of maps that had now been stuck up randomly on the walls, so that they could study them. There were St Cuthbert's ones drawn by boys; ordinance survey ones of the local area; old maps of countries, seas, counties and regions; and big scruffy looking maps covered with symbols and explanations that they had added on in different coloured felt tips. The overall effect, he saw now, was of mad, curling over, half unstuck wallpaper.

"So I see," said Mrs Sharp coldly. "And is this your usual classroom display, Mr Kay?"

"Well no, not exactly our display as such..." Mr Kay looked slightly alarmed by her tone. "More of a work in progress really; part of our learning. And actually, we're not in here that often." He attempted a smile.

"Oh, you have another classroom?"

"Not exactly. It's more that we're outside. That's where we're going now, in fact, to finish our orienteering. You see..." Mr Kay started to sound a bit more confident and adjusted his glasses. "We want to get a real sense of what north, south, east and west actually are. And how people have always found their way around. That's what we'll be doing this morning, using the humble compass

117

that has been used in navigation since the early eleven hundreds to find our way about. And tomorrow night," he was really excited now, "once it's dark, we'll be looking at how people found their way before, when they were guided – and still are, in some parts of the world – by the celestial bodies! The stars and the planets that move across the sky throughout the night." He smiled.

"I am well aware of what stars do, Mr Kay. What I am in fact interested to see is the actual work that the boys are doing this term. May I see their books?"

"We have all kinds of books on…"

"No. *Their* books, Mr Kay. Where they do their neat school *work*. Can I see one please?"

"Well the thing is," Mr Kay's smile was fading fast. "At the start of a project we don't do much actual writing, it's more a case of really getting inside and engaged with the topic, but from last term I can show you…"

"Is this one?" Mrs Sharp interrupted. She had picked up a rather grubby exercise book from a boy called Felix's desk, a boy who had gone home for a few days, and was holding it gingerly between her clicky long nails. *Ugh!* Jack shuddered. He hated those kinds of nails! How could anyone DO anything with those, except maybe scratch a blackboard? Actually, they'd be perfect for that. Maybe he could invent something that you could wear on your fingers…

Mrs Sharp began to flick through the book and from where he was sitting, Jack could see that the pages were full of tiny little maps, half drawings, symbols and more drawings, but no writing. And even if he hadn't seen, he would have known, because it was Felix's book and everyone knew that Felix couldn't write yet, though it didn't mean he was stupid, because he was brilliant and amazing at other things.

"Ah, that's Felix's, and you really must see some of the things he has made..." began Mr Kay.

"I am not here to see things that children have *made*, Mr Kay. I am here to investigate the standards at this school."

She put the book back down on the table with a slap. "I think I had better come back later, when I can look into things with due consideration. For now, please resume your class."

Mrs Sharp turned on her sharp little heels and marched briskly from the room, followed by the two guides. Giles turned and shrugged helplessly before he went out, and Mr Kay shrugged back. He looked worried. And Jack was too.

"Told you!" he muttered to Charlie.

~ ~ ~ ~ ~

Later that morning, Jack and Charlie were orienteering their way back from Clue Four, the pond, to Clue Five, which was something (*but what?*) closer to school. As they marked out their sixty paces to the north, a gang of wild and excited younger children from another class raced past in the other direction, cheering and whooping as they went. At the back, much slower, the last few were carrying a huge object, wrapped up in a bin bag. *What the...!?*

Jimmy, an Eagles boy, saw Jack and Charlie staring.

"Tell you later!" he called as he stumbled past with the load. "At the Den!"

And then they had gone.

Jack and Charlie looked at each other.

"I don't know what they're doing," Jack said, "but I'd bet a million pounds it's not something Mrs Sharp is going to like."

"Jack! You're driving me mad! Who cares about Mrs Sharp!" Charlie started counting his paces towards Studio 3. "And anyway, she's probably seen loads of good stuff today. She's probably doing something brilliant right now!"

At that exact moment, they glanced in at the open doorway of Studio 3 and were met with a terrible sight. Mrs Sharp, her face stricken, was rubbing frantically at a great green splodge on her jacket and shrieking up at Trudy to come down off the roof *for Health and Safety's sake!* Around her, boys dressed in oversized old shirts were painting an amazing mural on the wall while she wrung her hands and cried out *Stop! Please Stop! This is SCHOOL PROPERTY! Don't any of you understand?*

"Right, that's it!" Jack said to Charlie. "We've got to do something! This couldn't be going any worse. I told you what happens after a bad report. Everything fun gets stopped – and that includes Studio 3 Charlie! We've got to do something!"

"Okay," Charlie tore his eyes away from Mrs Sharp, who was even now wrestling a glue gun away from a boy who was about to stick his work together, crying out *No! Too dangerous!*

"You're right Jack. Let's go and find Mr Kay or Mr Bonham. They're the ones who need to know."

Ten minutes later, they raced into the hall and found Mr Bonham, in the middle of trying out the microphone with a few boys from another class.

"Testing! Testing!" his voice boomed and crackled across the great room. "And it's four hundred and ninety four for six and England win the ashes!" He raised his hands in the air, clutching an imaginary cup, and the younger boys all cheered. He spotted Jack and Charlie.

"Oh hello you two! Just setting the hall up in case we need an assembly. Mrs Sharp was reminding me this morning that we haven't had one for a while."

Jack and Charlie looked at each other. "Could we have a word with you about that for a moment Mr Bonham?"

But before he could reply, Mrs Sharp – red in the face and green-stained – slammed into the room brandishing her clipboard in the air.

"Mr Bonham! A word with you if you please!" She called out. "Your members of staff do not seem to understand the basics of Health and..."

But again, before anyone could reply, the double doors on the other side of the hall burst open and Edward – Ed –, the younger boy Jack remembered from his first day, rushed in, blood pouring from big scrapes on both knees and his face and hair wild. A small crowd of wild, excited looking boys followed him in, the ones he and Charlie had passed earlier.

"Goodness!" cried Mrs Sharp. "What on earth has happened here?"

"It's okay!" Edward cried out, oblivious in his excitement as to who Mrs Sharp really was or what she was doing there. He looked from face to face proudly. "I've been on Bomber 3. Down The Paths – the big one!"

There was a sharp inhalation of breath from a few of the boys in the room while those who had come in with

Edward nodded in support.

"What!" Mr Bonham climbed down from the stage. He was trying to look concerned as he came over, but Jack could see a similar light of admiration and... yes, excitement even...in his own eyes.

"And what, I would like to know, is Bomber 3?" Mrs Sharp's face was stern and all straight lines. She did not really want to know what Bomber 3 was. Or rather she did, but she had already decided it was something very bad. Her tone was distinctly *ominous*.

It reminded Jack of his mum's voice when she came across one of his cat experiments. Like when he left a tempting trail of tuna from the fridge to a picture of some mice, so he could finally find out if cats see pictures like we do. *And what, I would like to know, are you doing with that?* his mum had said. And she didn't mean *tell me all about your fascinating experiment!* She meant *That was for tea! I'm furious!*

But as Jack looked anxiously at Mr Bonham and the other boys he saw that incredibly, they hadn't picked up on this tone of voice at all. In fact, they were still looking at Edward who was even now elaborating on his adventure...

"What's Bomber 3?!!" he cried, full of passion. "It's only the fastest, bestest Go-Kart ever at St Cuthbert's. It's got swivel wheels at the front..."

"And bike wheels at the back!" a boy at Edward's side added.

"And the steering is some handle bars off a scooter!" the Eagles boy – Jimmy – piped up.

"But the breaks were never perfected!" Edward burst in. "And that's what makes it so risky." He paused, blood

122

still trickling down his knees, but full of pride. "And I've ridden it! I've done it! Bomber 3!!" He punched the air and the other boys cheered noisily.

"No brakes?" Mrs Sharp repeated, her voice cutting through the celebrations.

Jack looked despairingly at Mr Bonham. Couldn't he see what was happening here? Didn't he realise he was dooming the school? Mr Bonham was still smiling, but Jack noticed it was a bit less sure now (*at last!*) and he was giving Mrs Sharp some worried looks.

"No," continued Edward, blithely and full of joy. "That's the beauty of it! If you go down the hill path on Bomber 3, you know you're not going to be able to stop. At all! You have to stay on and steer...and those swivel wheels are dangerous! Or you have to throw yourself off – " he gestured wildly with his arms. "Like I did, near the bottom."

"But where did you get it?" Mrs Sharp was truly horrified now. "What about the guarantee? The manufacturers need to be contacted as soon as...."

"Oh we didn't get it!" Edward interrupted, happily. "We..."

"Perhaps Edward should go and get cleaned up," Mr Bonham suddenly interjected, "and I could show you the music rooms, Mrs Sharp?"

"...made it!" Edward finished, triumphantly. "Well, I didn't exactly make it. It was Dan and them a few years ago, when making a Go Kart was the Design and Technology Challenge? They've all left now. But they're legends at St Cuthbert's. Legends! They got the swivel wheels off a baby buggy. They didn't steal them or anything!" he added, noticing for the first time that Mrs Sharp was not sharing in any of the pride and joy, but was actually looking rather horrified. "No – they found them on the school trip. To the landfill site."

"Landfill!" Mrs Sharp sat down in the nearest chair.

"You know! Where all the mountains of rubbish go from all our houses and where it just rots and lies there for thousands of years and there's all those seagulls and bugs and diggers with caterpillar wheels?"

"Yes, yes..." her voice was faint now. She gazed blankly around her, as if trying to find her bearings.

"Teaching about recycling, you know!" Mr Bonham added hopefully.

But it was too late. Mrs Sharp was shaking her head, gathering herself, standing up and taking hold of her bag and her file.

"Go and clean yourself up child and get some help for those dreadful cuts!" she instructed, the steel back in her voice. "You boys take him. I don't think you realise how terrible it is that you fell from that Kart thing. You are meant to be looked after here."

"Oh it's not that terrible!" Edward called back proudly, as he was led bleeding from the hall by his friends. "EVERYONE falls off Bomber 3. This is nothing compared to some of the injuries I've seen!"

And he was gone.

A terrible silence filled the hall as the remaining people – Mr Bonham, Mrs Sharp, Jack and Charlie – all looked at each other.

"You will be hearing from us Mr Bonham," Mrs Sharp said, rather ominously, Jack thought. "Very shortly."

"Er... Could I not tempt you into seeing the art studio Mrs Sharp? It really is very popular with the boys and our resident artist is..."

"Yes, I believe I saw her earlier. On the roof, I think it was. No need, Mr Bonham, no need. As I said, you will be hearing from us shortly. Thank you and good day. I will see myself out."

And she was gone, the click of her heels echoing back across the hall.

The three of them stood there dejectedly.

"Oh dear...." Mr Bonham said, looking at Jack and Charlie. "I think St Cuthbert's might be in big trouble. Very big trouble indeed."

Thirteen

"Okay Jack, your turn!"

A strange flat feeling had come across the whole school since Mrs Sharp's visit. And so, as it was a Saturday and a strangely balmy day for October, Jack and the rest of the Eagles were over at the Den, trying to distract themselves.

Wilf, Angelo and several others were up on the platform under the tent roof, reading Bird Man. Zed was leaning against the tree's great trunk, idly sharpening another stick. And Vinnie, Charlie and Jack were further along by the swing, taking it in turns to swoop and sail over the very big drop, trying to decide if they were ready to jump off onto the mattresses below.

"I want to," Jack said, climbing onto the thick wooden stick that served as a seat. "And I don't want to." His stomach was churning just at the thought of letting go. But something in him desperately wanted to jump. And for days now, he had been swinging and thinking and shifting on the edge of the seat, always on the point of jumping off... but not able to make that final move.

"You'll do it when you're ready!" Wilf called down.

And that seemed to be how it happened with everyone. Many of the older ones had jumped by now, one by one, and each time there were huge cheers and congratulations. A few brave, wiry younger boys like Edward had done it too, the ones who were really good at climbing and other physical stuff. But lots hadn't got anywhere near. And even though all the boys shouted encouragement or called out *Go on! Do it!* or *Jump! Jump!* everyone seemed to understand that you didn't do it until you could, whenever that was. And the biggest force to get you to jump was inside yourself.

Out of everyone, it was Jack now who was almost ready, poised on the edge, with Vinnie not far behind. And this time he was going to do it. He was determined! He got comfortable on the seat and started to swing, feet pointing up to the trees on the way out, head facing down to the mattresses on the way back. Up and back, up and back, trees and mattress, until he was just in the right spot. Any higher and he would be too high… So now was the moment… Right now…

But not today.

He swung back down and got off, cross and disappointed.

"Never mind!" said Vinnie, patting him on the back. "I haven't done it either."

Jack gave a small smile and ignored Zed's smirking face over by the tree. Zed himself had declared he had no interest in jumping or swinging and would not even try. *I don't do physical stuff* he had said, with his usual disdain. *It's not my Thing.* And Jack had to admit he quite admired him for that. It showed a certain strength of mind and independence of spirit to not do what everyone else was doing.

Jack passed the swing across to a wild little red haired boy from Falcons who had dashed over to join the queue. He had done the jump days ago, when Eagles had let others join in. The boy leapt onto the seat, swung madly a few times and then pushed off with his hands, sailing down to the mattress far below. He landed in a sitting position and bounced happily before rushing back to the Falcons over by the pond. Jack sighed and grabbed the empty swing.

"Can someone tell me what's going to happen?" a voice shouted down from higher up in the tree.

It was Felix, the boy who had gone home for a few days. He'd heard about the inspection and been asking questions ever since.

"I mean," he shouted again, "I hope it's not gonna be my fault 'cos she looked in my book!"

"No way – it's not about that Felix!" said Wilf. "I've told you. It was everything. It all went wrong."

"But what's gonna happen?" he bellowed down again, sounding upset.

"Oh shut up Felix! " Zed shouted suddenly. Jack saw that his hands were white where he clutched his stick. "Stop asking such stupid questions. You're such an idiot! Nothing's going to happen."

"I only asked!" came a crestfallen voice from the tree.

"Leave him alone!" Jack said fiercely, much to his surprise. And, it seemed, to Zed's, who stared back at him.

"Yes, and it's not a stupid question," Wilf added, jumping down. "Felix is right. We need to find out more. It's been really weird the last few days, with the teachers

128

being all quiet and fed up. It's like the spirit's gone out of the school. We need to know what's happening!"

"I agree!" Angelo looked up from his comic. "I think we should just ask. Mr Bonham's good like that. He tells you the truth."

"Yeah!" Vinnie cried, hopping from foot to foot. "It's our school! We've got a right to know!"

"This is *exactly* what Giles from Kestrels was saying this morning," said Charlie. And then suddenly everyone was talking and shouting at once.

"All right!" Wilf raised his voice and held up his hand for quiet. "Let's find out. Who's on recycling duty with me? We can ask Mr Bonham when we go and get his paper."

Jack looked up. "I think it's me."

"Good" Wilf jumped down from the tree. "Let's go now. No point waiting."

"Yes now!" everyone shouted as Jack picked up his grubby Kerry Road sweatshirt from the ground. And suddenly it seemed the most urgent and immediate thing to do.

"Now!" the boys all shouted from the tree.

All except Zed who just kicked the great trunk with his foot.

"NOTHING is going on, I keep telling you all!"

~ ~ ~ ~ ~

"Mr Bonham?"

Jack and Wilf were poised on the threshold of Mr Bonham's study, recycling sack in hand, unable to bring themselves to go in. The curtains were drawn, the room was dark and Mr Bonham himself was slumped at his desk, head in hands. There were papers everywhere. He looked up.

"Oh hello boys," he said wearily, his hair on end and ink all over his fingers. "I'm afraid you've caught me at a low moment. Do come in." He gave a weak smile. "How can I help you?"

"We've come for the paper collection," said Wilf brightly. "It's recycling day! And also..." He and Jack glanced nervously at each other. "Also... we wanted to know, I mean, we wondered if you could tell us, what's happening? About the inspection? Some of us are worried..."

Mr Bonham smiled a little sadly. "Of course you are Wilf. I'm sorry. I really should have updated you earlier. I know how rumours can get about. But you see, I've been trying to research the facts and find out exactly where we stand." He indicated the papers all over the desk and floor before letting his hands fall back down in a gesture of despair.

"But I have no experience of this! I've been teaching all over the world until a few years ago and I'm just not up to date with the systems here. The last school I taught in was on top of a mountain in Guatemala and there was nothing like this! So when I opened up St Cuthbert's again..."

"It was you who bought the school!" Jack interrupted. *Mr Bonham rescued the building from the bats!*

"Well yes I did, Jack," Mr Bonham said, with a flicker of the old enthusiasm. "I did because I believed and I still believe that many children, particularly boys, learn better when they are active. They need to do stuff, experience stuff, get outside. Children have no problem learning when they are interested and involved, and when they are with adults who are interested and involved. How else did the human race get this far?"

He sighed and picked up a fossil from his desk and began to turn it over and over in his hands.

"But it's more than that. It's about having the chance to find out what you're good at and what you enjoy, so you can be your best self. It's good for you and it's good for the world. But most schools don't work like that you know."

I know! thought Jack, as he and Wilf waited patiently by the door.

"Look at grown ups!" Mr Bonham continued, putting down the fossil. "You get people who have passed every exam in their life and who earn lots of money working in a bank, when really they just want to make things out of wood, or be a nurse. And you get people making things out of wood who would have loved to be a teacher, and would have been a brilliant teacher, if only they had been given the chance. And worse than that, worse than unhappy people trapped in the wrong jobs, you get people doing nothing at all because they were told they FAILED at the school stuff. But they were never given the chance to find out what they *were* good at. So you see, it seemed such a good idea to start this school again..."

"It was!" said Wilf.

"Well yes it was!" Mr Bonham replied, but then he slumped again. "I just didn't realise what I was up against. And now, well, it's bad news. You might as well let everyone know because sooner or later they must. I think St Cuthbert's is in trouble and there's not a lot we can do. I'll be putting up a letter on the notice board later, from Mrs Sharp, so you'll all be able to read it yourselves. And of course I'll have to let parents know fairly shortly. But really, there's nothing much we can do. It's just a matter of waiting now."

He looked down at his desk and to his horror, Jack saw that Mr Bonham's eyes had filled with tears.

"If you wouldn't mind now Jack and Wilf, I need to get some things in order. Take the paper bin, take all of it, and let the others know. The letter will be up shortly."

They nodded silently. This was awful. And it was unfair! Jack had only had a short time at St Cuthbert's but he realised – possibly only in this moment – that he loved it! And now it was all going to change. And what about the other boys who were there all year? Surely it couldn't be about to end for them?

~ ~ ~ ~ ~

"Move out the way! I can't see!"

"Oi! Stop pushing! I can't see either you know!"

"I can't help it – it's Connor. Anyway, the whole school wants to know what it says you know."

All the boys were pushing and shoving to get near the noticeboard in the hallway and read the letter but no one could get a clear view, including Jack who was squashed against the wall next to it.

"What does it say James? You're at the front – read it out!"

"Yeah – read it James! Saves me pushing."

"All right. ALL RIGHT!" James – the boy with the bow tie – struggled to get free of everyone crowding behind him and cleared his throat. Everyone fell silent.

Dear Mr Bonham (he read)

Re: Preliminary Inspection Visit to St Cuthbert's School on Wednesday October 19th

My preliminary findings and recommendations are as follows:

1.1 Little evidence of good standards and outcomes for children at the school;

1.2 No test results available for scrutiny;

1.3 No clear identity: for example no school logo, uniform, or school gatherings such as assemblies;

1.4 Behaviour of many children – and several staff – questionable and inappropriate;

1.5 Entire school grounds and much of the school building breach health and safety legislation;

1.6 Children deemed at risk of injury and accident;

1.7 Risk of disease and infection from animals and plants at the school.

With regret, it is my recommendation that St Cuthbert's Wild School for Boys be closed down as soon as practicable.

A Senior Inspector will visit to confirm my findings. His recommendation will be official and final. Please get in touch with us to arrange a date, or we will come on a date chosen by ourselves.

There are of course actions that could be taken to address these findings at St Cuthbert's but it is my opinion that this route would prove far too costly and take many years. I highly recommend that you abandon any such thoughts and close the school. Alternative schooling will need to be found for the boys back where they live.

With all good wishes

B Sharp

Mrs B Sharp
Advisory Inspector to the Senior Inspectorate

James's voice fell quiet. No one spoke.

Jack turned to look at all the boys who were grouped around the noticeboard and filling the hallway, and at others who were sitting all the way up the staircase or hanging over the bannisters above. Their faces, their eyes, their thoughts, their feelings, all matched his own and there was nothing to say.

The inspectors were going to close the school!

Fourteen

"But there must be a way to make things better!" Vinnie protested. "She c-can't just c-close the school."

Jack, Vinnie, Charlie, Wilf and a few other boys were sitting in the common room, too fed up to play games or make anything or talk about anything else. Zed was in an armchair nearby, reading a book on Second World War Military Strategy. Similar groups of boys were gathered together here and there in the big room and in the other common room, slumped in chairs or talking about what had happened.

"Course she can Vinnie," said Charlie. "Jack was right to be worried about the whole thing. But Mr Bonham will think of something! He'll find a way round it!"

"Or he'll ignore it!" said Vinnie. "Do his own thing!"

"Well..." Wilf looked at them all. "I hate to tell you this but I think he's already found out what he needs to know."

"What? What do you mean?" They all spoke at once.

"I'm sorry Jack," Wilf said, turning to him a little apologetically. "But after I left you, I looked at some of the papers from Mr Bonham's bin. I know I shouldn't have!" he added hastily. "But I couldn't help it. I thought it might tell us something."

"Well what did they say?" Charlie asked, eyes wide.

Wilf took two crumpled pieces of paper from his pocket and smoothed them out on top of the table.

"Here," he said, pushing them towards the other boys. "See for yourselves."

They crowded round to read.

SAFETY SURFACES R US!

Dear Sir

Thank you for contacting Safety Surfaces R Us! You have just made the first important step towards protecting your children from broken arms and legs or FAR WORSE.

We at Safety Surfaces R US passionately believe that no activity – no matter how fun or educational – is worth a single child suffering bumps or scrapes and we are committed to eliminating any such risk. For good! We give you our word!

For installation of safety surface matting throughout the woods within the grounds of St Cuthbert's Wild School for Boys (approx. 2 square miles): £5 million + VAT
Approximate time scale of works would be four years.

We trust this quote meets with your approval and look forward to carrying out the works forthwith.

With kind regards and remember – nothing is more important than absolute safety!

Ian Bradshaw

Head of Sales

The boys looked gloomily at each other and turned to the second letter.

Kiljoy and Liveless Ltd

Sir,

We are a small, family run legal firm specialising in legal action following child injury during play.

Child fallen off a rope swing? Twisted an ankle jumping off a low wall? Let us help! We will press charges against your school or local authority and GET YOU A PAY OUT!

We helped the following children and their families:

LUCY, aged 7, was playing jump on the kerbside next to her school and she tripped and twisted her ankle.

MATTHEW, 10, fell off a rope swing put up by older boys in his local park and broke his arm.

TAYLOR, 5, badly scratched his throat eating cornflake cake at the school breakfast club.

We can't change the tragic accidents that happened to Lucy, Edmond and Taylor. But we can flatten kerbsides, ban rope swings, ban puddings, ban anything!

And we can make sure that schools and parks and shops are so scared that they are to blame for these accidents, that they'll pay you anything to keep quiet, and never risk a cornflake cake again.

Killjoy & Live-less – There's always a way!

"What!" said Vinnie. "What does all that mean?"

"Basically," Wilf collected the papers and folded them up, "it means the only way to keep St Cuthbert's open is to pay five million pounds to cover over all the ground in the woods with that safety matting, like they have in parks..."

"The school can't pay that!" Charlie said. "And Mr Bonham would never agree to cover over the woods!"

"Or," Wilf went on, "to ban us from going on the grass or doing any other fun or risky thing at all..."

"He wouldn't do that either!" Charlie cried. "These letters were in the bin weren't they!"

"But if he doesn't do those things," Wilf said calmly and patiently, "Mrs Sharp and the lawyers could close it down or take him to court. They could do that just for what happened to Ed on Bomber 3, let alone anything else that happens here! And that's not even looking at everything else Mrs Sharp said about exams and uniforms and all that stuff."

Silently, they absorbed this information.

"Yeah," said Charlie eventually, thoughtfully. "My uncle used to have an ice cream van and someone tried to take him to court 'cos they slipped on a Choc-Ice wrapper and hurt their leg. They said it was his fault! It finished his job for him."

"Yes, that's about it," said Wilf, looking round the others. "It will probably mean the end of St Cuthbert's and back to our old schools for all of us."

"Oh man!" Charlie flopped back in his chair. "Not Dalton again! They hate me there!"

"What about me!" The dots of Vinnie's freckles stood out from his pale face. "I'll have to sit in school all day again and I'll go c-crazy. What if my letters go bad again and I c-can't talk like I c-can here?"

"And I'll be back to endless competitive exams," said Wilf, smiling sadly. "Or maybe a different special school. But it won't be one where I can feel normal and even clever! At least you've only just got here Jack and you're leaving anyway. It will be easier for you."

Jack had been so caught up listening to the others that he hadn't thought of himself yet. But he did now. He thought greyly of Kerry Road...

"I could have asked to stay longer..." he said, realising how much he wanted to. "It's just my mum who wanted me back."

"Oh shut up!" Zed shouted suddenly from his chair, throwing down his book. "Shut up all of you!" And he slammed out of the room, his cloak billowing behind him.

Jack looked questioningly at the others.

"His family don't want him at home," said Wilf, quietly. "They're loaded with money but they don't even come and get him in the holidays. He practically lives at St Cuthbert's. If he has to leave, where will he go?"

~ ~ ~ ~ ~

That night, Jack lay in bed unable to sleep. The room was dark, the others were fast asleep and Jack himself was tired. But for some reason he just couldn't drift off as he usually did. His mind was full of problems and disappointing things.

He just couldn't believe that St Cuthbert's was about to close! Unless something drastic happened or changed, he was going to have to leave here after only a few weeks as planned, with no chance of staying longer or coming back because the school would be gone.

And that meant back to Kerry Road... He could see that grey and gritty road again now, waiting for him to scoot down; the school gates and Mr Clipper with his bell; the playground where he couldn't do anything; the lessons where he was no good; the week-ends stuck at home arguing about computer games because he didn't want to do sports. And though he wanted to see his mum and Ellie, he just didn't want to give up the colour of St Cuthbert's, not yet...

For a start, he still had so much to do! Maps, night orienteering, the rest of the autumn study. His conker was only a twelver. The Eagles' Den still needed perfecting. And they'd only had one English lesson round the fire!

But more than that, he still didn't know what he was good at yet, or even if there *was* anything...

And what about friends? He would really miss Charlie and Vinnie and Wilf and some of the others. And being part of the Eagles. Even Zed, who was mean, was at least easier to understand now that Jack knew what he came from.

And he still hadn't jumped off the swing! Or been to the Paths! They were banned following Mrs Sharp's visit, which meant he was probably never going to get a go on a bike there either...

Dad!

Suddenly he saw him in a way he had not remembered for years: loaded with cycling gear, on the bike he loved, grinning and waving goodbye as he free-wheeled down the hill where they lived, off on his great cycling adventure. No one had said to wave extra hard! Or to carefully remember that scene! No one had said he wouldn't come back!

But he never did. And Jack had never seen him again. He couldn't even properly remember what he looked like. Only if he looked at photos, or sometimes in dreams...

Oh Dad!

"Jack?"

A little later the door opened a crack and a line of light spilled onto Jack's bed. It was Mrs Hopewell, in her dressing gown.

"Are you all right? I heard a noise as I was checking on you all before I went to bed."

She crept quietly over to the bed and sat down on the edge. "Are you sad?"

The light from the door lit up the lines in her face. She looked kind and tired.

Jack nodded his head a tiny bit.

"I know." She stared off at the wall. "Your mum told me about your dad. It still gets me about Mr Hopewell too sometimes, especially at night. He died quite a few years ago now, like your dad. But I still miss him you know. You never stop missing that person."

Jack didn't move.

"I know it was when you were very little Jack but it's okay to still be sad you know."

Another tiny nod.

And then, remembering what his mum had always said but for the first time really feeling it, he said, "But he died doing something he loved. My dad was happy on his bike."

Mrs Hopewell nodded. "It's good to know that, isn't it." She gently patted the duvet close to Jack. "Very important to know that."

They stayed there in silence for a little while, Jack lying unmoving on the bed, Mrs Hopewell sitting on the edge. Finally she sighed.

"You try and get to sleep Jack. You need your energy for the day. And the way things are going, there may not be many days left at St Cuthbert's." She smiled a little sadly and heaved herself up on to her feet. "Sleep well."

The door closed and the light disappeared, along with Mrs Hopewell's steps. For a moment Jack thought he saw a movement, over in Zed's direction.

Oh no! Did he hear?

But when he looked, the shape under the covers was still and all was quiet.

Jack turned his face to the window again, relieved. And now, through the gap in the curtains, he saw the sharp, thin crescent of a new moon, like a silver comma in the sky.

It was the last thing he saw before he slept, and dreamt.

And when he woke, he had an idea.

Fifteen

"Anyone for bacon sandwiches?"

Mrs Walker stood red faced and aproned in the dining room, looking around at the gloomy faces before her. Some boys were eating cereal, some were nibbling toast, others were just staring out of the window or slumped in their chairs.

"Don't all shout at once!" she said grumpily, turning to go back to the kitchen.

"I will, Mrs Walker!" Jack came skidding into the room in his socks, pulling his Kerry Road sweatshirt over his head, his hair still wet from his shower. "I'm starving!"

"Good!" she beamed at him. "At least one of you is eating properly."

Wilf and Angelo stared at him.

"What have you got to be so cheerful about suddenly?" asked Angelo dryly. "Or have you forgotten. The school's going to be closed and we're all going home."

"I know that," said Jack eagerly, taking a seat and waiting a moment while Mrs Walker put a plate of bacon sandwiches in front of him. "But I've got a plan!" He took a big mouth of white bread and butter and bacon.

"What kind of a plan?" Wilf asked half-heartedly.

"Well," Jack swallowed and considered. "The kind of plan that is a bit tricky and a bit unlikely but if it works... well, it could make a difference."

"To the school?" said Wilf, leaning forward slightly.

"Well, basically, yes," said Jack. "It all came from something Mr Bonham said, about the most important thing at St Cuthbert's..."

Wilf and Angelo looked at each other.

"Tell us more."

~ ~ ~ ~ ~

"Later today," Mr Kay said, walking between the desks, "we're going to start something a bit different, something with a historical slant." He paused and looked out of the window.

"Pssst!" Felix hissed from Jack's right. "Pass it on!" And he handed him a rather grubby looking note.

"Using the library and other resources at the school," Mr Kay continued, "I want you to find out three things about the past life of St Cuthbert's. Any three things, but it must be about the school in the past."

Jack already knew what the note would say, and it did:

Eagles Emergency Meeting 3pm today at the Den. All must attend!

He smiled and passed it along to Charlie.

"But what is the past?" Sam P was asking. "I mean, how far back does it have to be to be the past. Does yesterday count?"

"Good question!" Mr Kay smiled. "And actually, yes, yesterday is the past! But I want you to find out things from further back than that. So let's say, for the purposes of this project, that the past means over ten years ago. Yes Joe?"

"Mr Kay, how can we find out this stuff? We haven't got a computer."

"Yeah, you'd be able to find out so much more on a computer!" Sam P called out.

"Yes, well, we don't have that here," Mr Kay went on. "So you need to think what other resources there might be. Let's call it a research topic. Or a detective task! And you have the next week until the end of term to do it and hand in what you find out.

But for now, I want to finish the measuring work for our map project. So, get your stuff together and let's go out." Jack saw the note move back round behind him and he smiled again.

~ ~ ~ ~ ~

"Okay," said Wilf. "Can everyone hear?"

"YES!"

It was 3 o'clock, the tent sides were rolled up and Eagles boys were crammed onto the main platform of the Den, some of them sitting and some of them standing. Others were wedged onto branches or perched on smaller platforms down below, where they could still see what was happening. A light drizzle was falling and coating the heads of anyone not under the canvas roof.

"Well, thanks for coming to the emergency meeting everyone. And as you have probably heard, we have a plan."

Wilf held up his hand to stop the cheering.

"But, I'm not going to tell anyone what it is yet, because the fewer people that know about it for now the better."

The groans made him hold up his hand again. "Sorry, but that's how it is. This is only Stage One. If this works, you'll all be told about Stage Two. I'm going to pass you across to Jack now. He's devised this plan and he needs to recruit some people to help. We need the best people possible for each bit. So be honest with yourselves. And later on – if there is a later on – everyone will get the chance to help."

Jack sidled forward from the spot where he had been standing nervously next to the tree's great trunk. He looked around the platform and below at the expectant faces turned to face him and cleared his throat.

"Well, for tonight, for Stage One, that is…"

For a moment, his words died away. But he took a deep breath and focussed on his idea. "For tonight, this is what we need. First, we need someone who gets on well with Sarah in the office who can find a way to get her to leave the room unlocked when she goes home at half past four."

There were murmurs and then several voices called out "Ben, she likes you! She thinks you're cute!"

"She doesn't!" Ben, the boy with the big brown eyes, cried out in a stricken voice.

"She does!"

"Well I'm not doing it!"

The boys near Ben laughed and poked him. "Cutie pie!"

"Okay," said Wilf, swiftly. "Anyone else?"

"Well what about you Wilf?" said Angelo. "She trusts

you. You're the oldest boy in the school. And you're a kind of leader."

"Yeah that's true." Other boys were nodding. "You do it Wilf."

"Well," said Wilf, considering. "Okay. I'll come up with a good way to do that. What's the next thing Jack?"

"We need someone to keep watch tonight while we do what we need to do. Someone with quick reactions who can keep their head."

"Oh me, me!" shouted Vinnie. "I'm very quick! Let me do it."

"But can you keep your head, Vinnie?" Wilf asked.

"I promise I c-can!"

"Vinnie, you *are* quick," said someone from the back, "but Joe would be better at that job."

"What!"

"Well, he's quick, but he's quiet too."

"Yeah – it's true Vinnie," said Charlie. "You're so good in sports situations but Joe is quick AND quiet. He'd be better here."

"That's not fair, I…"

"Okay!" Wilf raised his voice again. "Look, this isn't about what we want to do. It's about who would be best. Vinnie, you'd be the first to be picked if this involved running or scoring anything. But I agree that Joe suits this job more. If you're happy to do it Joe?"

Joe nodded, pleased under his long hair, while Vinnie humphed a bit with folded arms.

"Okay good. Joe it is to keep watch. Jack?"

"Then," resumed Jack, feeling a bit bad for Vinnie but carrying on. "We need someone who is *really* good at writing. In different styles."

"What do you mean?" asked Felix.

"Well," Jack considered, "someone who could write a letter in, say, a teacher's voice."

"Sam P!" everyone called out.

It was true. Sam P was a good writer. He had written many of the Bird Man stories and he did well in English. Where Jack had got good comments from Mr Bonham for his ideas, his writing and spelling had not been great. In fact, it was bad. But Sam had got brilliant comments for his writing.

"That okay with you Sam?" Wilf asked.

"Yep!" Sam P punched the air, pleased to be chosen.

"And finally," said Jack, "I need someone who is very good on computers."

There was uproar. "ME! ME!" everyone shouted at once. "Let me do it!"

"NOT games!" Wilf called out, and the shouting died away.

"Research!" Jack added hastily. "We need someone who can find out information really quickly and who can get into emails, websites, that kind of thing, and then get out again. Without leaving any trace."

"You mean like a hacker?" Jimmy, sitting at Jack's feet, sounded excited.

"What's a hacker?" Ben looked up at the older boys.

"Someone who uses a computer to break into other people's computer stuff illegally," Wilf explained. "But it's not quite that. Well actually, I guess it is quite like that." He looked worried for a moment. "But it's for a good purpose – kind of like Robin Hood!"

This reassured everyone. But there was still silence. No one knew how to do this.

And then, from a branch next to the platform where he had been lounging without interest, Zed tipped back his top hat and spoke.

"I'm pretty good," he said. And then, as all faces turned to him, "I was excluded from my last school for it."

A wave of interest swept over the boys as everyone called out *Why? What did you do?*

"It doesn't matter," Zed shook his head. "But believe me, I can do anything you need on the computer."

There was silence while Wilf and everyone considered him.

"But what about how you've been lately Zed?" Wilf asked. "You've been horrible to a lot of people and lost your temper loads recently. Are you going to be like that if you come?"

Zed swallowed. It was the first time Jack had ever seen any sign of anything bothering him at all.

"Well, I'm... sorry about that," he said, finally. "I just don't want St Cuthbert's to close. And if this might keep the school open, I'll do it. And I'll do it well."

Wilf and Jack looked at each other. What other choice did they have?

"Let's give him a chance," said Jack.

"Okay good," Wilf nodded. "That's settled then. Joe, Zed and Sam P, stay here with us and we'll go over our plans for tonight. The rest of you..."

Wilf raised his voice as everyone started to shift and stand and get ready to go: to climb, to play, to run, to swing...

"...make sure you say absolutely nothing to anyone! Not even friends in other teams! If this gets back to any teachers, we'll be in serious trouble. And we'll lose our only chance to save St Cuthbert's."

~ ~ ~ ~ ~

Midnight. The luminous face of Jack's watch showed the time clearly. Exactly on cue, there was a soft knock at the door and Wilf came quietly into the room.

"You both ready?" he whispered.

Jack and Zed nodded. They were sitting on the edges of their beds, dressed in their darkest clothes. It had been a long evening to get through and no one in the room had been able to sleep. Charlie and Vinnie had passed the time by telling stories about St Cuthbert's and to Jack's surprise, even Zed had joined in with a few funny tales.

"They've been ready for hours!" Charlie said now from his bed. "You sure you don't need an artist for this bit?"

"Yeah!" Vinnie bounced into sitting position. "Sure you don't need me too?"

"Sorry Charlie, Vinnie," said Wilf. "But if we find anything good in this bit, there'll be lots to do for Stage Two. And be quiet will you! Mrs Hopewell will hear you! Ready Jack? Zed? Sam and Joe are waiting in the corridor."

They nodded and stood up to follow Wilf.

"Good luck!" hissed Charlie as they left.

Sixteen

Outside the room, the corridor was lit by a low night-light. The boys, joined by Sam P and Joe, trod softly along the wooden floor in their bare feet, conscious of every wheeze and squeak of the boards as they went.

"Good luck, whatever you're going to do!" came a loud whisper from one of the rooms as they passed.

"Great!" hissed Wilf. "We've been heard already!"

"Only 'cos they're listening out for us," Sam P replied. "Everyone is. But Mrs Hopewell won't be."

They carried on until, at the end of the corridor and through the doors, they found themselves in front of her room. Jack thought briefly of the night before, when he and Mrs Hopewell had been awake, thinking of their people who had died. Was she awake now, thinking of Mr Hopewell?

They all stared at the door, willing there to be nothing. Jack thought he could see a low light inside but there was no sound, no movement. They were okay.

The boys proceeded to the head of the stairs and began, one by one, to tiptoe down. *Like in a cartoon*, Jack thought. *We should have that music they always play when people are tiptoeing along in a film.*

Then, exactly like in a film, Wilf stopped unexpectedly towards the bottom of the stairs and all the other boys banged into each other, with whispered shouts of *ow!* and *what's happening?*

"Shh!" Wilf said, holding up his hand. "I heard something."

They stopped dead still and quiet, and listened. There was a faint *tap, tap tap...* getting louder and closer...

And there was Zoe, standing foursquare in the hallway, looking up at them. She was a tiny dog with little legs but if she barked now and woke Mrs Hopewell, or Mr Bonham in his apartment, they were stuffed! The boys held their breath. Zoe regarded them slowly, taking them in almost one by one, and then tap tapped to the bottom of the stairs to be patted. She knew them! It was okay! They breathed a collective sigh of relief and made to carry on.

Silently, Wilf indicated to Joe to stay at the bottom of the stairs with Zoe, where he could watch every possible entrance into the hall. Joe nodded. He knew the drill. If anyone came he was to have a coughing fit and say he had wandered down looking for water. Not a great reason to be downstairs, given the taps upstairs, but better than his initial sleep walking idea, which they all agreed was a bit far fetched. Hopefully, whoever found him would take him back upstairs, leaving the others warned and free to make their escape.

Wilf tried the handle of the office door. Open! He smiled and they slipped silently into the room, closing the door behind them.

"Phew!" said Jack quietly, looking round the darkened office. "How did you manage it Wilf?"

"I said I'd left my homework in here when she was leaving and she leant me the key. I'll lock up and put it back after. Now, let's get on with it. Zed, your turn!"

A gap in the curtains let a strip of yellow into the room from an outside light and it lit up the desk in the window place and the old, square computer crouching on top.

"I'm amazed it even works!" Zed whispered, as he sat down in front of the screen.

But they knew it did because Wilf had done his research. Sarah used the computer for *school administration* and that was it. *Mr Bonham never uses it* she'd told him. *He's got his own email address and everything but he never checks it. Drives me mad!*

Zed pressed the power button and then, quick as lightening, turned down the sound as an irritating tune pinged out to announce to the whole school that the computer was on. They looked at each other in horror at the noise. Jack knew, and the others knew, what very great trouble they would be in if they were caught in here. Big, serious trouble, not like anything he had ever had before.

And yet, they had to try something, didn't they?

The screen lit up and icons appeared and everyone sighed in relief. Now they could put their plan into action! From that moment, Jack directed.

"Okay, Zed, get into Mr Bonham's email account."

Click tap click. They were in. There were hundreds of messages that had never been opened, all looking very business-like, and Zed scrolled down the recent arrivals to try and see if there was one about the inspection.

There was an email from Killjoy and Live-less Solicitors Ltd, no doubt following up their letter. One from Safety Surfaces R Us! with the subject line saying SAVE TWO THOUSAND POUNDS ON OUR LATEST QUOTE! And one from something called Prohibitions Ltd that offered CHEAP *KEEP OFF* AND *KEEP OUT* SIGNS! in the subject line. Then, finally, a few down, one from Mrs Sharp.

"There it is!" said Jack. The subject line read:

PROPOSED SENIOR INSPECTION 01142, ST CUTHBERT'S WILD SCHOOL FOR BOYS.

"I feel funny looking at his emails," Sam P whispered.

"I know," Wilf looked serious. "But it's only this one. And it's only because he doesn't. And it's our only chance."

Zed clicked on it.

Dear Mr Bonham (they read)

We need to arrange a date for the Senior Inspector, Robert Fanshaw, to visit St Cuthbert's.

We have not heard from you with a date. I would like to suggest we do this as soon as possible, so that both you, your staff and all the parents can be clear about the future of the school and, assuming you are not able to reach the standards we require, the boys can begin to be placed back in their local schools.

Therefore, unless we hear from you, we will be arriving on Wednesday 29th October.

We look forward to seeing you then.
With best wishes

Bertha Sharp
Advisory Inspector to the Senior Inspectorate

"*Bertha!*" said Sam P, stifling a laugh.

"Never mind that! What about the date? That's in a few days isn't it?" Wilf looked at Jack.

"Okay," said Jack slowly. "But before we do anything about that, we need to do some research on Robert Fanshaw. Who is he? What's he like?"

Zed was already tapping and clicking on the computer, typing in the senior inspector's name and searching through what came up.

The first link he found was to a local council page, showing a dull black and white photo of a man in a suit. Hang on – it wasn't black and white. *He* was! Grey hair, grey suit, white shirt... there was just nothing of any colour on him or about him.

"Doesn't look very promising," Wilf said.

"Let's read what it says." Jack wasn't ready for defeat yet. They were all briefed about the plan and knew what they were looking for.

"Nah, there's nothing there we can work with!" Sam P was a quick reader and had already scanned the paragraphs below the photograph. "It's just about his different jobs in the... what is it again? ... the National Schools Board Inspection Department, over the past twenty years."

"Okay," said Jack. "Anything else Zed?"

Zed tapped some more and they followed another link, this time leading to notes from an Inspection Department meeting about how best to present school inspection reports.

"Nothing here."

Jack sighed. His plan was beginning to look too hopeful.

"Try again," he urged Zed. Zed frowned and tap tapped into another link, this time a YOU! NETWORK page in the name of Robert Fanshaw. There was another photograph of the same man, in colour this time, and in Union Jack swimming shorts, doing the thumbs up sign.

"This looks more hopeful!" whispered Jack, leaning closer. "Does it link to any writing? We want stuff about him as a person, not about his job."

Zed tapped onto a couple of links and suddenly they were on his YOU! NETWORK personal page, meant just for his friends.

Yo dudes! Just updating my personal profile! I'm married to Joanna now and we have two children who are 4 and 6. I'm still an Inspector – a Senior Inspector in fact, which I never expected, or really planned for! I can't say I love it. In fact, I can't say I even like it. But at least I have a job!

I still find time to do my sea swimming. Once a year I usually get to go.

Favourite food is still sticky toffee pudding… Love that stuff!!

Those of you from my schooldays will remember my old dream to be an artist… I was pretty good, even if I say so myself. Not much time for any of that anymore. Funny how all those childhood dreams and ideas kind of go…

Bingo! The boys looked at each other excitedly. This was it! This was what they needed! And so exactly what they needed that they almost couldn't believe their luck!

"Well done Zed!'" said Wilf, grinning.

"Yeah, well done," said Jack.

Zed looked back at him. "Well done to you Jack. It was your idea."

For a moment they almost smiled at each other. Then...

COGH COGH URGH URG COH!

What the...! The boys looked at each other in horror.

COGH COGH URGH URG COH!

"Could be a real cough?" suggested Sam P in a tiny whisper. But then a light switched on outside and flooded under the doorway, freezing them where they stood, and Mr Bonham's voice boomed around the hallway.

"What on earth are you doing down here Joe?"

"I was... I was just coming to get water Mr Bonham. I've got this terrible... COGH COGH URGH... cough."

The boys were silent and unmoving in the bluey light of the computer, frozen into their last shape. Why was Mr Bonham there? What would he do next? There was no reason why he should come into the office... but the computer was on, the screen was bright and humming loudly and even their breathing seemed loud. And why was Joe downstairs looking for water when there were taps upstairs?

And who on earth coughs like that?!

"We forgot to ask for a good actor!" Sam P whispered. Jack and Wilf silenced him with hard stares.

"Water! But why didn't you get some upstairs?"

"Well...COGH, UGH... I just couldn't stop coughing and

COGH UGH it's so echoey in the bathrooms. I didn't want to wake anyone. COGH"

"I see. Well that's thoughtful of you Joe. But are you sure this is about a cough? I couldn't sleep myself you know, what with everything that's going on at the moment, worrying about what will happen to all you boys. Most of you will be all right, I'm sure. But some of you... Are you sure it isn't about that rather than your... um... cough?"

"COGH! UGH!"

There was silence. It was so hard to work out what was happening when you couldn't see anything.

"Very well. Let's go upstairs to Mrs Hopewell. She'll get you a drink and maybe a cough sweet. Would that help?"

Joe must have nodded, because the next sounds were of them climbing the stairs and a few whispered voices floating back down the stairwell as they went.

"Right! We've got minutes!" said Jack. "Sam, write an email to Mrs Sharp and tell her to come on the date she suggests. We can be ready by then. Make it sound like Mr Bonham. And ask them both to stay for lunch!"

Seventeen

"Well? What happened? Did it work?"

Several Eagles boys were gathered around the breakfast table where Jack, Wilf, Joe and Sam P were eating breakfast, half an hour late. They were all pale and tired, with dark circles under their eyes. Jack for one still hadn't quite got over their close escape. They'd had to wait ages in the office before being sure Mr Bonham had gone back to his apartment!

"It's definitely on," said Wilf, chewing some toast and jam. "We're doing our history projects this afternoon but tell everyone to meet at the Den again at 3 o' clock. We'll give instructions for the next bit. And by the way, get some boys from the other teams. We're going to need everyone at St Cuthbert's to be in on this or it won't work."

"Even then..." said Jack, not wanting everyone to get their hopes up. He was getting a bit worried about the responsibility of being the one with the plan. But then, seeing the crestfallen faces around him, he added, "But it's the best shot we've got!"

~   ~   ~   ~   ~

"Mr Bonham?"

Jack stood clutching his clipboard in the Headmaster's open doorway, trying not to notice the papers still spread everywhere and the slightly dishevelled look of the man as he sat as his desk. It didn't look like he had slept much either.

"Ah Jack. Hello. How are you?"

"Okay thank you."

Mr Bonham stared at him for a moment. "You know, Jack, it must be a bit strange for you to come here and then suddenly have all this... upset and confusion. I'm dreadfully sorry about that. Though I suppose you were due to go back to your old school soon..."

His voice trailed off. "Anyway, what can I do for you?"

"Well," Jack sidled into the room. "I was just wondering if you could help me with my history project. Mr Kay wants us to find out three things about St Cuthbert's in the past. All the other boys are doing their own detective work..."

"Oh really!" Mr Bonham perked up slightly. "How interesting. What are they doing?"

"Well, Charlie is sketching some of the old parts of the building, 'cos that's his Thing. Some of them have gone to the library 'cos there's lots of old local history books there apparently. Some others are looking at Mr Kay's maps 'cos there was definitely one of the school area about a hundred years ago..."

"Yes, that's right, there is. Very good. And how can I help Jack?"

"Well..." Jack hesitated. "You said the other day that it was you who bought the school again a few years ago, after it closed? It was you who rescued it from the bats?

160

I thought you might know stuff. About its past. I thought I could just ask you."

Mr Bonham smiled and tapped his pencil on the desk. "Yes, that's true. Primary research is a good approach, Jack, going directly to people who are involved. But what kind of thing do you want me to tell you?"

"Just… about it really. What the school used to be like? Before it got closed? If you know, that is."

Mr Bonham remained silent for a while and then said thoughtfully, "Come in properly Jack and close the door. That's it, just move those papers and take a seat. I was saving this for round the campfire but I might as well tell you now, seeing as you've asked. And seeing as we may not sit around that campfire again."

Jack sat down, pen and clipboard at the ready, wondering what Mr Bonham was going to say or how it would help his history project.

"I bought the school Jack," Mr Bonham sat back in his chair, "as you know, after it had been closed for years. I think everyone knows that. But what most people don't know is that, many years ago, I actually came to this school, when I was a boy."

Jack's mouth dropped open slightly. "You came to St Cuthbert's?"

"Yes," Mr Bonham smiled at Jack's surprise. "We all did. All of the Board members. We were one of the last groups of boys to go through the school before it was closed down. And we were the luckiest group in many ways, because we were here when it was at its most different and at its best. Are you taking this down by the way?"

161

Jack blinked and looked at his clipboard. "No. But I will."

"Good. Now where was I? Oh yes, the school. Well, before the war – the Second World War – St Cuthbert's was a very exclusive boarding school, for the wealthiest boys only. It had the best teachers in the country, the richest and most privileged pupils, the most beautiful grounds... And it had been like that for several hundred years. It was widely considered to be the greatest thing if you could get your child into the school.

But the War changed all that. The War, as you must know, brought difficult times to the country. Many children from all over London and other cities needed to be evacuated from their homes and sent to the countryside, so they would be safe from the bombings, and many men including teachers had to go off to fight."

Jack nodded. He did know about that.

"But difficult times often bring unusual solutions, Jack, and at this time it was proposed by the very patriotic school board that St Cuthbert's should help with the war effort. It was decided that the school would welcome boys who had been evacuated from the cities, for free, regardless of their background or whether they had any money. At the same time, to fill the shoes of teachers who had gone off to war, the school would advertise for anyone with an interest or a passion who could come and help inspire the pupils.

It was at this lucky time that Rupert and I joined the school. I can see you are wondering, so yes, I do mean Rupert John Woolacroft, my best friend and the man who recommended you to St Cuthbert's. He is also, incidentally, John of the boat story. I know, you are surprised to hear about these different versions of the man you met in the café, and there is a lot to tell of his adventures. But that is for another time...

Rupert and I were the greatest of friends and from similarly wealthy and protected backgrounds. So to come to St Cuthbert's at this time of fewer rules, different boys, wilder play and interesting people as teachers was both a joy and a challenge that ultimately set us on the right path for life.

We were lucky! While men fought for our country and for freedom and equality for all, the difficult war years actually gave us an opportunity we would never otherwise have had. We made friends with boys from all over England and beyond, we explored and played wild games endlessly, we listened to teachers who had their own interests and passions to tell us about, and we learnt a lot. Far more, in fact, than if we had been at St Cuthbert's as it was before. We learnt how to play, take risks, push boundaries, solve problems and get on with each other. We also learnt about our own strengths and weaknesses, our own interests and passions, and we began to discover *our things* in life!

And I must tell you here, Jack, that there is not a limited *thing* for each person in the world. It's more a process that goes on throughout your whole life, as you uncover and discover what it is you enjoy, what you are good at and what makes you tick.

And so, this process underway for Rupert and me, we left school prepared for life and keen to contribute to the world in the best way for each of us. And that is the history of St Cuthbert's and why I have opened it along those lines again today."

Mr Bonham sat back and looked at Jack, his eyes shining and his face alight. He laughed and it was nice to see that laugh again.

"Will that help with your history project Jack?"

Jack nodded, grinning.

It's going to help with a lot more than that.

~ ~ ~ ~ ~

"Okay, Stage Two! Jack, do you want to talk everyone through it?"

Once again Eagles boys were crowded excitedly onto the Den platform and on the branches below. This time there were more boys, as representatives from Kestrel and Falcon had come to hear the plan and then report back. There was also less noise, as someone had brought a huge bag of large, fruit chews from home and everyone was still at the stage where the sweet was too big for their mouths and too hard to chew properly.

Wilf shuffled back so Jack could shuffle forward and face the audience. He was less nervous this time and had thought a bit about what he wanted to say.

"Okay. Stage Two. First, I'm going to tell you what we need, because we only have two days to sort this out. Then I'll explain the plan and we can decide who does what."

He glanced round at the chewing faces looking up and across at him and felt a tremor of worry. They were all relying on his idea to save the school! His glance caught that of Zed, sitting on his branch, rather more attentively than last time but still lounging compared to everyone else. He raised his top hat slightly.

"I have to just say that this may not work!" Jack blurted out. "It's a long shot! A wild idea! I don't want everyone to get their hopes up..."

"Don't worry about that Jack." Zed, one of the few people to have refused a sweet, spoke up from his branch. "No one else is doing anything. It's the only chance we've got. So we might as well go for it."

Jack looked at him, surprised and grateful.

Most boys nodded, chewing steadily.

"And if it doesn't work," said Sam H – one of the Falcon representatives – rather thickly. "At least we tried!"

"Yeah – we've got to try!" shouted Charlie.

Jack nodded, reassured. "Okay – I just wanted to make sure. But, if we're looking for positives, I can tell you we've got history behind us."

"What do you mean?"

"What history?"

The faces around him looked puzzled.

"I'll tell you that in a minute, but I'm just saying, this school has had difficulties before. Big difficulties. And they found a way round it. So maybe we can. Plus, it's really worth fighting for. But I don't need to tell you that."

Most people had finished their chew now and there were several cheers. Jack felt encouraged.

"There aren't any schools like St Cuthbert's. We can't let it close without a fight. We have to try and use our brains, our initiative and our team-work to see if we can save this school!"

The cheers were bigger.

"And who knows, we might just do it!"

The cheers were so loud that no one could hear Jack

speak. When they died away, he focussed in again with renewed confidence.

"Okay then. This is what we need. Firstly, everyone needs to find black clothes to wear." He looked around at the nodding faces. This at least was not going to be a problematic request.

"Secondly, I need people who are really good at singing and music." There were whispers amongst the crowd and Jack knew that there were plenty of boys who fitted this.

"I need someone who gets on well with Mrs Walker the cook..."

At this, there were shouts of *Tommy! Tommy!* from the Kestrel boys, referring to a skinny little boy in their team who ate all the time, and whom Mrs Walker made it her personal mission to feed well. Jack smiled.

"Okay, good. Then we need some red and white danger tape. You know, like they use to fence off accidents or no-go areas? Some road traffic cones. Oh, and some pork chops, uncooked. And a group of artists to be working in Studio 3. In a minute I'll ask who can do what. But for now, I want to talk you through the plan. Listen carefully and take it in. We have no time for mistakes."

~ ~ ~ ~ ~

It was the end of the day.

While Charlie, Vinnie and a big group of boys were excitedly discussing the plan, Jack slipped out of the common room. His head was buzzing and full of all the many details, as well as a growing sense of responsibility to all the boys and the whole school. What if the plan failed? What if it had no effect whatsoever? Everyone kept telling him not to worry, but he did.

And then, for some reason, in the middle of his crowded thoughts, he realised he wanted to be alone. So now he made his way down the darkening stairwell, grabbed his coat from the cloakroom and headed out of the back door of the school.

Immediately, the fresh, clean-cold air revived him and he began walking towards the Den and the woods. It was the end of an autumn afternoon and in front of him the sky was a glowing mixture of red and pink and gold as the sun came near to setting. Against this deep colour, the woods were silhouetted sharp and black, with many branches standing out against the sky, and the wood birds – *rooks* he thought they were called – were cawing noisily.

Jack walked slowly, looking, listening, feeling. It felt good to breathe in the air and see the sky and be alone with his thoughts. The buzz in his head began to dissolve outwards into the autumn air and the autumn air begin to enter his whole body until eventually, it was like he and the evening were one thing. He felt light and happy.

This is the first time I have ever walked alone, freely, in the natural world.

He stopped. It was as if the words had come from somewhere else, not from him. Yet at the same time, he realised they were utterly true. And just what he had been missing.

Eighteen

Keep pedalling Jack! Keep holding on to the handlebars and looking straight ahead!

Jack was on his first ever bike without stabilisers. His dad was behind him, pushing him along.

I am! Jack shouted back, feeling the bike wobble as he tried to cast his words over his shoulder but managing to ride straight ahead. *Don't let go!*

I let go ages ago Jack... His dad's voice was further away now. *You're doing it on your own!*

Jack woke with a start and looked at the clock: 6.45am. Inspection day. Everything was planned, everything was in place, there was plenty of time. But still he felt sick with nerves. He took a deep shaky breath.

I need to go outside alone again.

Leaving aside the clean, black clothes laid out on his chair, Jack pulled on some rather grubby old ones and his trainers and slipped out of the room, down the stairs and out into the still dark morning. To warm up, he ran steadily towards the Den. Behind him, the sky was beginning to lighten to grey but ahead of him all was dark.

At the edge of the woods he paused and then headed in, crunching through the leaves that covered the ground until he got to the ancient oak tree. He sat down on the damp ground and leant his head back against the gnarled old trunk, looking out across the drop to the woods beyond, in dark and in peace. He sighed and closed his eyes. He already felt so much calmer and less worried.

Why have I never done this before? But then, when and where could he have done any such thing at home?

"Woke up early did you?"

Jack span round, eyes wide. *What the...?!*

Zed was sitting, wrapped in his cloak, further round the giant tree trunk. Jack fell back in relief against the tree.

"You made me jump, you idiot." He grabbed a stick from the ground next to him and threw it away into the gloom.

"Sorry," Zed said. He did, for once, look genuinely sorry. "I sometimes come here when I can't sleep."

"It's okay." Jack sat back again. " I just thought I was alone. Hey, how come I didn't notice you weren't in our room? How long have you been out here?"

Zed shrugged. "Twenty minutes? I'm not sure. I wanted to come and sit by the Den, before it all... you know."

Jack nodded and his hand found another small stick next to him. He began to scratch away at the soil.

"Do you really not know where you'll go? If St Cuthbert's closes I mean."

"Oh I'll go somewhere!" Zed said tonelessly. "My parents will make sure of that. They'll track down another expensive school for me, in another place, and I'll have to start all over again. But nowhere will be like St Cuthbert's. And not many places want you there in the holidays, so..."

He trailed off and stared into the trees. Jack stared too, taking this in. There was nothing to say really. What could he say? He chucked his stick.

"You're really lucky you know," Zed said. "Not... not in some ways, I know..." he added quickly, looking embarrassed suddenly. And Jack wondered again, *did he hear me last night?*

"I mean," Zed looked more comfortable again, "being able to go home. Having a home."

"But you must have a massive house!" Jack burst out. "Your family are rich aren't they?"

"Loaded," Zed said flatly. "And our house is massive. And the grounds are too. And we have a pool, and my mother has horses, and we have holiday houses in Switzerland and Italy..." Again a hard smile. "I said *home*, Jack, not house."

Jack stared at him. "But..."

But what? Again, he didn't know what to say. It was true! At least he, Jack, would go home to his mum and Ellie, and others who he liked, even if it would mean school days back at Kerry Road. He leant against the tree again and sighed.

They sat in silence for a while. And then the sky began to lighten and a first bird began to sing in a tree nearby, and it was a beautiful, sweet sound.

"Dawn chorus!" said Zed. "When the birds wake up. You should hear it in summer. It's deafening!"

They were silent again, just listening.

"Let's just do our best today to keep St Cuthbert's open," said Jack eventually. "We need to, so you can stay. And so I can ask to stay longer. If I don't, I'll never find my Thing. If I've even got one that is!"

Zed turned to him in surprise. "Don't be silly. Your Thing's obvious! Well, one of them anyway."

"Is it?" Jack was baffled for a moment. *He had a Thing?*

"Of course! You're an ideas man Jack. A real ideas man." And Zed smiled, the first proper smile he had ever given him. "Come on, let's get back and put your biggest one into action!"

~ ~ ~ ~ ~

At nine o' clock precisely a dark grey car came slowly up the drive of St Cuthbert's, crunching and flattening the gravel in front of the school. It parked, neatly, and both front doors opened. Mrs Sharp emerged from one, pulling down her dark blue jacket and straightening her hair. A very tall man in a grey suit unfolded from the other.

"It's Mr Fanshaw!" said Sam P. "I recognise him from the website. He's tall!"

Jack, Sam and Wilf, smartly dressed in black, were huddled round one of the front bedroom windows, looking down at the gravel where even now Mr Bonham was meeting the guests.

"Come on!" said Jack, turning away and pulling at the others. "We need to go down."

The boys raced along the corridor and down the stairs, slowing on the last flight so that they would be the first people to greet the visitors as they entered the building.

"Oh... Jack, Wilf, Sam... Good timing!" Mr Bonham came through the door with the guests, looking a little worried. "You remember Mrs Sharp, don't you? And this is Mr Fanshaw, the Senior Inspector for this area. He's come to... er... look around the school."

Wilf stepped forward and held out his hand. "Nice to meet you Sir, Madam." He shook hands with them both, as did Jack and Sam.

Mr Fanshaw, tall and a little stooped, gave a small smile, but otherwise his expression was very hard to read. *Inscrutable,* Jack thought. Wilf turned to the guests.

"We're just on our way to morning assembly if you would like to accompany us?"

Mr Bonham looked rather taken aback by this and Mrs Sharp also looked a little surprised. It was not what either of them was expecting, and one of them was meant to be the Headmaster.

"Ah good! An assembly," said Mr Fanshaw, not noticing any confusion. "I do think it's a good way to get a first impression of a school. Lead on!"

Wilf and Sam P took charge, leading the two inspectors through the double doors into the hall while Jack dropped back.

"Mr Bonham," he whispered to the Headmaster, who was looking a little puzzled. "We've planned some things today, to show the best bits of St Cuthbert's. I hope you don't mind letting us do them..."

"Well I..."

"Please! It might make a difference. We've sorted it all out. And we thought it would be really good if you could tell the visitors a bit more about what St Cuthbert's is all about. In the assembly, you know? 'Cos we haven't had one for a while."

"Well...yes, I could do that part, certainly." Mr Bonham nodded. "All about St Cuthbert's you say? Why not! I will." He pushed open the big double doors. "Might as well have my swan song eh!" he added over his shoulder.

But then he stopped in his tracks. "Good Lord" he said under his breath. And even Jack was astonished by the sight.

The room was full of rows and rows of uniformed boys, dressed neatly and almost identically in black. *Almost!* Here and there Jack could spot an odd clothing item or some rough edges or some frankly weird outfits. But it was good enough! And as they sat, so still and to attention, the sweet sound of singing filled the room as the choir – all the boys in the school who loved music! – raised their voices, singing the end of the hymn Jerusalem.

Bring me my bow of burning steel
Bring me my arrows of desire
Bring me my shield of righteousness
Bring me my chariots of fire.

Jack had never really listened to the words before but now, standing near the door with Mr Bonham and hearing it sung so clearly for the first time, he heard them.

I will not cease from mental fight
Nor shall my sword sleep by my side
Till we have built Jerusalem
In England's green and pleasant land.

As the last words died away, a profound silence filled the hall before someone – Robert Fanshaw! – started to clap. And then everyone else joined in. Even Mrs Sharp, eventually. And as if called by the sound of applause, Mr Bonham leapt onto the stage, clapping the choir as he went, ready to address the room.

"Welcome everyone to this special assembly at St Cuthbert's Wild School For Boys," his booming voice rang out, as the clapping died away. "Special because, although we have so many talents and gifts at this school, we so rarely get to show them off. And today we are very proud to do so."

He gazed around the room.

"A particular welcome to our two guests, Mrs Sharp and Mr Fanshaw. We hope you enjoy your day here. And as you are here to find out about St Cuthbert's – to inspect us, in fact – let's take a moment together to examine just what this school is all about. Because it's worth examining beneath the surface, it really is."

Mr Bonham's voice had that confident ring and lift to it again! *He's going to do a good speech* thought Jack, as he slipped out of the hall again. He had a few things to get ready for the day and the assembly was in safe hands.

He made his way to the back door of the school, Mr Bonham's words growing fainter and fainter, and ran through the autumn air to where Vinnie was waiting for him, holding red and white danger tape and hopping from foot to foot with impatience.

"They'll be another five or ten minutes in there," Jack called out. "Let's get the tape up as quickly as we can!"

Vinnie needed no prodding and together they ran over to the edge of the woodland that hid the Den and unravelled the tape, tying it to sticks that the boys had spaced out the night before. It was a quick job and by the time they were done, it looked as though the whole woods were out of bounds and unused.

"I've locked Zoe in the junk room with a pork chop,"

said Vinnie. "That'll k-keep her out of sight and stop her yapping."

"Any left in case we need them later?"

"Yep – I put them in a bag in the Den. On that first platform."

"Okay good. Is everything else ready?"

"Far as I know."

They smiled at each other.

"Okay," said Jack. "Back to assembly!"

Breathlessly, Jack and Vinnie slipped back through the hall's double doors, just in time to hear Mr Bonham finishing his speech.

"So why send a child to St Cuthbert's?" he asked the room. "Not to get the best test results. Or to look good to people on the outside. Or even – forgive me – to please inspectors.

No, our aim is to help boys rediscover that spark of learning they have within themselves and nothing less will do. What do they like doing? What are they good at? What excites them? Find these things – be it art, sport, food, maps, writing stories, or anything else – and the interest and the will to learn will be there. It WAS there, ladies and gentlemen, before they ever went to school. And somehow, for some children, it gets lost.

And why do we need to find this? Because we want all children to learn well and have happy, productive lives, of course.

But also – and this is important – because what the world needs most right now is people who are creative, motivated, enterprising and confident; people who can make things happen; people who can contribute their unique gifts to the world. Because it is those people, in the end, who will create better communities and a better world. Welcome to St Cuthbert's!"

As a roar of applause greeted his final words, Mr Bonham left the stage. Jack looked across at the visitors. Mr Fanshaw, he noticed, was looking rather thoughtful.

But there was the whole day to get through yet.

Nineteen

Ratatatat.

At ten thirty, the knock came. Two guests entered Jack's class, this time led by Wilf. Tall, stooped Mr Fanshaw came first, his face still inscrutable, followed by short Mrs Sharp.

She looks like she's just drunk lemon juice, thought Jack.

"Don't mind us!" Mrs Sharp announced to the room. "You just carry on."

Jack saw a muscle twitch at the side of Mr Kay's mouth but he gave the visitors a little nod and carried on talking to Charlie about his work.

The Eagles were in the middle of their first piece of written work for their mapping project. Jack was writing about explorers and pirates and the merchant navy and how they had all found their way around the seas of the world. He then planned a story about a stow-away on a boat, with a map of an invented treasure island. He was looking forward to illustrating it with very detailed pencil diagrams.

The visitors began to wander around the classroom, looking at what boys were doing.

"If you would like to look over here," Mr Kay interrupted, "I've set out all the work that last year's class did around mapping, so you can see how the whole project unfolds and how we learn at St Cuthbert's."

Mrs Sharp wrinkled her forehead. *She could screw her hat on*, thought Jack.

Mr Fanshaw approached the table.

"We take an idea you see," Mr Kay began to explain, "like mapping, and the first thing is always to get children to experience it in real life, ideally outside. Once they're interested and it feels real and meaningful to them, they'll want to learn about it. Only then do we move on to writing and classroom learning."

Mr Fanshaw nodded in an interested way and Mr Kay adjusted his glasses, encouraged.

"We always involve lots of subjects together in a project – art, science, history, maths – and we make sure there are lots of chances for children to have their own ideas."

"And what," interrupted Mrs Sharp, icily, as she approached the table, "about children whose reading and writing are poor? Isn't it a complete waste of time to have them gallivanting around outside, when they should be working on their letters?"

"On the contrary," said Mr Kay, patiently. "The best way to get boys to want to read and write is to get them interested in what they are going to read and write about. We're very good at that here. Didn't Mr Bonham tell you? But we value other skills and talents as well. No one feels a failure at St Cuthbert's. Look at this. This is what Felix made earlier this term."

Mr Kay un-scrolled a large and beautiful map, drawn in detail in colourful inks. It looked like an artist or professional mapmaker had made it, over many months.

Mr Fanshaw looked at it for a long time. "That's wonderful. Where is Felix?"

Felix, hair on end and wearing what looked like a rather dusty black dress over some black trousers, put his hand up from his desk by the wall.

"Did you learn a lot from this topic Felix?"

"I learnt all of it! I just can't write it yet."

"Well your map is wonderful."

"I know."

Felix was not exactly modest. But it didn't matter.

"Felix was the boy whose book you looked at last time Mrs Sharp," Mr Kay could not resist adding.

~ ~ ~ ~ ~

Lunchtime. The smell of fish pie wafted through the dinner hall and most children were already eating.

As far as Jack could tell, from talking to others, Mrs Sharp and Mr Fanshaw had spent the morning with different classes. Falcons reported the visitors sitting in on their maths lesson where they had set up a shop and were using real money to do sums. And Kestrels class were visited whilst they were finishing their autumn project. There was only lunch and then Studio 3 left to see. But here were the visitors now and, as planned, the only spaces were at Jack and Charlie's table.

"Well," said Mr Fanshaw, sitting down. "This smells good."

Mrs Walker placed a steaming plate in front of both the inspectors. "Home made fish pie," she announced, "with the last of our own grown spinach."

"Mmm!" Mr Fanshaw tucked in. "Fresh green vegetables! Very healthy. So, why don't you boys tell us the best thing about St Cuthbert's." He took his first mouthful. "Gosh, this is good!"

Mrs Sharp, sitting next to him, began carefully unfolding her napkin.

This was Charlie's big moment but he was rather caught up in his lunch and a tense silence fell across the table. Jack kicked him hard.

"The best thing for me," Charlie said, swallowing quickly, "is art. And Studio 3."

"Art eh? Interesting. And why's that young man?" Mr Fanshaw paused in attacking his fish pie.

"Well…" Charlie considered. "The thing about art is that nothing can be wrong. It's just what you want to make. And if it doesn't feel right or you make a mistake, you can turn it into something else. And sometimes, that something else is even better than what you were trying to do in the first place! Plus you can just keep trying 'til you get it right. I love drawing and painting and making things for everyone to see. It's just my Thing."

"Well I understand what you're saying," said Mr Fanshaw, "I used to love art myself. In fact…"

"But what about when you're older and you need to get a job?" interjected Mrs Sharp, who was picking through her pie in search of bones that were not there. "What then? Of what use will art be to you exactly?"

Jack felt a little pang of alarm but Charlie was unfazed.

"Well. There's a very interesting fact that Mr Kay told us," he said, waving his fork around. "Did you know that 65% of the jobs that everyone in this school will be doing in the future have not been invented yet? And lots of the ones you *do* know about won't exist at all! Maybe even yours, Mrs Sharp!"

Mrs Sharp blinked at him.

"And," continued Charlie, "everyone will probably change jobs ten or twenty times in their lives. So, to my mind, I'm better off doing what interests me and what I'm good at. And if there isn't a job to fit it, I can invent one!"

"I really don't think…" began Mrs Sharp.

"Yes," Vinnie interrupted. "Mr Bonham always says that the most important thing is to have ideas and to be able to change and stay interested. That way, whatever jobs are invented, we'll be able to fit!"

Mr Fanshaw nodded, chewing his final piece of fish pie. "Yes, that is an interesting way of looking at it. Our current school system certainly has some outmoded elements to it…"

Mrs Sharp looked furious and Jack felt a surge of hope. Things seemed to be going their way!

At that moment, Mrs Walker arrived with the pudding.

"Sticky toffee!" she announced, triumphantly, placing the bowls of spongy custardy syrupy stuff in front of them, where they gave off a hot, sweet, steam.

"Ah!" said Mr Fanshaw, closing his eyes and inhaling. "My favourite!"

~ ~ ~ ~ ~

Jack approached Studio 3 with some trepidation. Charlie and the guests had gone over there earlier, with the rest of the class, and Jack was going to join them. He'd just been checking on Zoe. The Studio 3 experience was so essential to the whole inspection going well that he was almost too nervous to go in. He decided to go round the back of the building and look through the window first.

He started down the path to the gardens and then doubled back so that he was behind the Studio and edging along its back wall. There was a tree stump next to the wall and Jack climbed on to this and then, putting his toes in the shallow gap between bricks, hauled himself up to look through the window.

At first, he couldn't make out anything; the windows were so smeary from years of weather and paint splatters. *I must tell the Management Team* he thought. But, once his eyes had adjusted, he saw clearly.

Mrs Sharp was sitting on a chair in the corner, staring at something in a state of what appeared to be shock. But what? Jack looked round the room. Zed and a few other boys were having a meeting, their chairs in a circle, and various comic work was spread out on the floor around them. It couldn't be that. Charlie was working on his canvas, a huge colourful and painstakingly detailed picture of everything he liked. It couldn't be that. Could it?

And then Jack saw Mr Fanshaw! He was... well... He was in the middle of the room, in overalls, covered in paint, and kind of dancing around.

What the?

Jack craned closer to the window and could just about make out his words through the glass.

"...Yes! Yes! Oh this is wonderful! Wonderful! How did I ever forget that paint flows in my veins!"

He rushed to a canvas and kissed it, and then pranced round the room again. Everyone appeared to be ignoring him, but Jack could see this was only with supreme effort. Most were trying not to laugh. Apart from Mrs Sharp, who was staring in horror.

This is it! This is what we wanted! Jack thought. He nearly fell off the wall with excitement. *Mr Fanshaw has remembered the learning that he loved and forgot! He's re-discovered his Thing! Art!*

Jack was so lost in the view through the window that he didn't hear anyone approaching. He jumped at a sharp tap on his shoulder, losing his shaky grip on the window ledge and falling on to the wet grass below, next to someone's black and shiny shoes. He looked up. Mr Bonham!

"A word with you please, Jack? In my study?"

Twenty

Jack followed Mr Bonham back into the school, his heart sinking with every step.

He knows! He's found out about the computer. The plans. All of it!

They went into the study, now cleared of papers, and Mr Bonham sat down at his desk, gesturing for Jack to sit in one of the other chairs.

"Right," he said, sitting forward. "I don't know what you've planned Jack, you and the others, or what you're doing...No!" he held up his hand as Jack went to speak. "Listen to me. I don't want to know. It would be worse for me and worse for you if I did. But I want you to tell me now, is there anything – as Headmaster of this school – which I really ought to know? Or can we let this day unfurl and be what it will be?"

Jack took a deep breath and gathered his thoughts. He thought about what they had done in the office. Should he tell about that? No, best not now. What about their plans for the day? No point now. Anything else?

"Well... there are a few things you could do in the bit of time that's left that might make today go better..."

he said hopefully, looking carefully at Mr Bonham. The Headmaster raised his eyebrows, as if to say *carry on*.

"Well, it's just, everything must impress Mr Fanshaw and what he's interested in, 'cos he's the one that makes the final decision. That's why we wanted him to go to Studio 3, 'cos he loves art and wanted to be an artist."

"But how did you...?"

"But Mrs Sharp's got it in for us, I don't know why. She hates St Cuthbert's."

Mr Bonham nodded. He'd realised that bit at least.

"And she keeps trying to remind Mr Fanshaw of what's wrong with it and how it doesn't fit all the rules and everything."

"Yes, the rules..." Mr Bonham said, with a touch of the old despair returning. "There are so many of them. It's all so different to when I taught here before, before my time in the Guatemalan mountains. Children would skip and run to school there you know. And beg their parents to let them go."

He sighed. "Still, now is now. And you boys might be interested to know that Mr Kay and I have in fact been working on getting all the paperwork together for the inspectors, as we knew a second inspection was coming at some point, though we didn't know it would be today."

He looked suddenly and piercingly at Jack, who shuffled awkwardly in his chair.

"How did..?" He shook his head. "Anyway," he continued, "we can show how boys were doing at their old schools, compared to how well they are doing here. And it's very positive! I knew this already of course, but having proof will help."

Jack nodded. That sounded good. It really did seem like they were on track to convince the inspectors!

"Okay," said Mr Bonham leaning forward. "That's all I need to know for now. Apart from one more little thing, Jack. Can you explain..." he smiled his old smile, "what, exactly, you have done with my dog?"

~ ~ ~ ~ ~

As the school day came to an end and most of the boys returned to the common rooms or were playing on the small area of gravel out the back, a small group stood outside the large front entrance: a paint spattered Mr Fanshaw, an increasingly angry Mrs Sharp, an eager Headmaster, and Jack, Charlie, Sam P and Wilf, the boys who had been involved in showing the visitors around.

"I must congratulate you on Studio 3," Mr Fanshaw said happily, shaking Mr Bonham's hand. "I've had a wonderful time in there. Wonderful! What an incredible resource for the school. It reminds me of my own happy days in the school art rooms..."

"Thank you," said Mr Bonham. "We at St Cuthbert's do believe..."

"Excuse me!" Mrs Sharp burst in, icily and purposefully. "But I have almost had enough of this!"

Everyone stared at her.

"If I may be allowed to interrupt for one moment and return to our agenda, there really are some serious issues we still need to address according to the inspection criteria. I trust you remember that is why we are here, Mr Fanshaw?"

"Well yes but..." Mr Fanshaw started to look a little uncertain.

"I have several issues to raise before we depart. I trust you have no objection to my doing so Mr Fanshaw, given that that is actually our job today?"

"Yes, of course..." Mr Fanshaw brushed awkwardly at his paint-splattered suit and searched in his pockets for a pen.

"The first issue I would like to raise," Mrs Sharp continued, with a righteous light in her eyes, "is computers! You talked about jobs in the future young man," she turned to Charlie. "But answer me this! Out of those 65% new jobs, how many do you think will involve computers?" She gave a cold, hard smile. "A large proportion, that's how many! So why doesn't St Cuthbert's teach computer studies?"

Jack and the others looked at each other helplessly. What could they say? It was a good question.

"As Mr Fanshaw will be aware, section 4(a) part iii of the inspection criteria clearly states that all schools should be teaching computer studies. It is a vital, VITAL, part of this brave new world you keep referring to, Mr Bonham. Even I, who barely use technology, can see that."

Jack's spirits sunk a little lower, as did everyone's. Mrs Sharp was right! Even Mr Bonham, who was passionate about why St Cuthbert's didn't have computers, was silent, gathering his thoughts. *Surely*, thought Jack, *we're not going to fail now?*

"And secondly," she went on, before anyone could respond. "The woods! They're dangerous! Are they used by boys or aren't they? Because if they are used for anything other than learning with a teacher, they are seriously breaching Health and Safety law for all schools. Isn't that so Mr Fanshaw?"

Mr Fanshaw, looking a little more stooped than before, brushed anxiously at more of the paint on his suit.

"Oh, the *woods*!" Mr Bonham stirred suddenly into action, throwing a quick glance at Jack. "The woods! Yes, um, they are totally out of bounds, as you can see by the… er… emergency tape clearly demarcating the er… danger zone. And even before we realised our terrible Health and Safety error…" his eyes met Jack's again, as if to say *forgive these fibs!* "…they were only ever used for the gentlest of nature walks."

A picture flashed into Jack's mind. A picture of fires and stories, Dens and swings and tree houses, of running and climbing and jumping and inventing and building and solving and swinging and flying.

"Well that's all right then!" said Mr Fanshaw, relieved.

"But is it true?" said Mrs Sharp, loudly. "Because if it isn't…"

At that moment, Jack heard the piercing but unmistakeable sound of a small, yapping dog hurtling towards them through the school hall. *Oh no! Not now!*

"Zoe!" Mr Bonham called out joyously, in spite of himself. "I mean… Oh! It's that stray dog that keeps coming round here. I think it lives over there somewhere…" He gestured vaguely towards the school meadows.

"Good lord!" exclaimed Mrs Sharp. "It's that terrible dog I told you about Mr Fanshaw. The one that was here when I last visited. It definitely lives here, Mr Bonham, you told me so yourself!"

Zoe scampered straight up to them, but went past them, and then back again, yapping incessantly and pulling towards the grass.

"It wants us to follow it!" cried Mrs Sharp. "It wants to show us something over there!"

Oh no! thought Jack, horrified. And he saw Wilf and Charlie realising the same thing. They all knew what she wanted. *More pork chops!*

Zoe raced towards the red and white tape, circled back, and barked at them, waiting for someone to come.

"Follow her Mr Fanshaw!" cried Mrs Sharp. "I can't go on that mud in my heels. Find out what's going on! There's something in the woods she wants you to see! Go on man!"

Reluctantly, tall paint splattered Mr Fanshaw set off at a slow jog to follow Zoe, while the group of boys watched him heading ever closer to the woods, the Den, the tree house, the swing and the million other signs that the woods were alive with play and use and adventure.

"I don't know what you'll find, Mr Fanshaw," Mrs Sharp called after him triumphantly, with relish even. "But I can guarantee it wont meet school Health and Safety laws!"

She looked at the silent faces around her and then she screeched, "This school's closing down! It's finished!"

~ ~ ~ ~ ~

It felt like hours passed as the small group waited for Mr Fanshaw to return.

No one spoke to Mrs Sharp, who stood a few paces away, writing things in her notebook. No one spoke to each other either. They were all too nervous. And the longer Mr Fanshaw took, the worse things looked for St Cuthbert's.

At last, they saw him coming back slowly across the field, Zoe trotting at his heels.

It's all over, thought Jack. *He's found it. The school's closing down.*

"Well, he's certainly been a while," Mrs Sharp said pointedly, happily even, echoing Jack's thoughts. "What can he have found! It's not looking good for you all..."

But as he drew closer, Jack saw to his astonishment that although Mr Fanshaw was walking slowly, he was smiling to himself. A kind of secret smile. And as he approached the driveway, he gave a little wave.

"Well, Mr Fanshaw?" called out Mrs Sharp, sounding a little irritated. "What did you find?"

"Find?" he repeated, a little dreamily. "What do you mean?"

"For goodness' sake man, are the woods used or aren't they? What did you find over there?"

"Nothing!" Mr Fanshaw replied, calmly and clearly. "Absolutely nothing."

Jack, Wilf, Charlie, Sam P and Mr Bonham all looked at each other in astonishment.

"Nothing?" Mrs Sharp repeated, looking a little bewildered.

"That's right. You heard what I said. Nothing. There is nothing whatsoever to report on in those woods."

Mr Fanshaw pulled down his jacket and stood up straight to his full height. "So I think, Mrs Sharp, that you and I will now be on our way. We have seen enough. We will be writing to you of course, Mr Bonham, with our decision. And I need to tell you that as the Senior Inspector – " and here he looked hard at Mrs Sharp, as if to say *that's me, buddy, not you* – "my decision will be final. I cannot tell you all now what it will be. I need to go and reflect on the many, different things that I have seen and then make my decision. But I promise to notify you very shortly."

And with that, he turned to the still frozen Mrs Sharp and gestured to their grey car.

"Shall we?"

But as he turned, Jack noticed something strange. Something that gave him a small amount of hope. He looked at Wilf and Charlie to see if they had seen it too.

For stuck to the back of Mr Fanshaw's grey and now crumpled suit jacket were a few dry and broken leaves and twigs, and streaking the length of his long grey trousers were the unmistakeable traces of muddy grass stains.

Twenty-one

"Nothing whatsoever to report on in those woods! I still c-can't believe he said that!" Vinnie, sitting across one of the armchairs in the common room, was still amazed. "I mean, that was *so* c-close!"

The other boys nodded. Jack, Charlie, Wilf, Joe, Sam P and Zed were all on chairs near the radiator, going over the story of the inspection day yet again. Other groups of boys were dotted around the room, playing cards, talking, messing about, reading and eating sweets. They had heard it all many times too. But it was this group, this group that masterminded the whole inspection, that couldn't tire of it.

"I know!" said Jack. "It felt like HOURS we had to wait there with Mrs Sharp. And she was *so* glad we were going to get caught out..."

"Miserable, old..." Charlie started to say.

"*Nothing in those woods...*" Vinnie repeated, laughing.

"I know!" said Wilf. "But even though he didn't tell on us, Vinnie, we still don't know his final decision. It could go either way."

The boys were silent for a moment, wondering. Zed

stared out of the window.

"But you really saw twigs and stuff on his c-clothes?" Vinnie asked for the tenth time.

"Definitely!" said Jack.

"And you really think he went up the tree house?"

"I know he did!" Charlie said with certainty.

"And the swing?"

"'Course!" Charlie was adamant. They all were. "He was a boy once wasn't he?"

~ ~ ~ ~ ~

"So, my friends…"

Mr Bonham, holding a rather formal looking letter in his hand, gazed at everyone in the hall. Pupils, parents, brothers, sisters, grandparents… all were gathered here, full of tea and cake and sandwiches, staring up at him expectantly for his final address before the holidays, waiting to hear the important result of the inspection.

"So," he said again, in his booming voice. "I received the final letter and report from the National Schools Board this morning. And I have been waiting until now to formally announce the serious news it contains."

Mr Bonham's face was expressionless as he unfolded the letter and Jack felt his heart thudding in his chest. Every boy in the hall craned forward in his seat.

"And I can now tell you…"

Yes? thought Jack, and every other boy. *Yes?*

"…that despite being twice inspected – or perhaps precisely *because* we were twice inspected – St Cuthbert's Wild School for Boys will NOT close. We will remain open!"

Jack leapt to his feet and cheered, along with all the other St Cuthbert's boys in the room. He grinned happily across at Charlie. *This is the best news ever! And Zed is going to be so relieved!* He turned to look for the familiar top hat and cloak. Where *was* he? He hadn't seen Zed all morning.

But Mr Bonham was talking again.

"For now at least!" he shouted over the cheering, as people sat and quietened down. "And I need to tell you that we have been awarded…" He looked down at the letter he was holding, "…the status of *Specialist Outdoor Learning Academy Focussing on*… Well anyway, we can stay open everyone!"

There were huge cheers again.

"And as I wrote to the National Schools Board this very morning, what better way to ensure that children care about nature and the future of our planet than to let them play and learn in it! You can teach as many lessons as you like *about* the environment, but if a child has never played alone or with friends outside, interacted with trees, watched a bird build a nest, or even just seen the sky and how it changes, how will he or she ever really want to help save the natural world? Let alone all the other learning that comes from these things."

Jack looked up at his mum, sitting next to him and clapping, and she glanced down at him. They smiled. *Could she, would she, give him more freedom after this?*

Then he gave Ellie, on his other side, a friendly nudge. She was clapping and stamping and cheering along with everyone else, though Jack wasn't sure if she knew why she was doing it.

It was so good to see his family. Everyone at St Cuthbert's had come into the hall that morning to meet up with their relatives who were already gathered there, so all the reunions happened at the same time. Boys called out to brothers and sisters, hugged mothers or fathers and in some cases grannies and grandads, and everyone was talking at once. That suited Jack just fine. He didn't want to be watched while he hugged his mum and Ellie, and his mum's face was wet with tears, and Ellie was dancing around singing *Jack's back in the bunk bed, Jack's back in the bunk bed…*

And now, here they all were in the hall. Charlie was sitting in the row in front of him, with his mum and what looked like four little Charlies ranging in size from the one Jack knew, right down to a toddler sized version in a red woolly jumper, all of them wriggling around and poking each other. Over the other side of the hall, Wilf was sitting still and quiet with a tall blonde older sister and two tall blonde parents, listening intently to Mr Bonham. And Vinnie and his dad and sisters were in the row behind, chattering away in loud whispers. There was such a happy feeling in the hall, of celebration and end of term and holiday and reunion, all rolled into one.

But where on earth was Zed?

"There are two final things I want to say about this before we break up for the holidays!" Mr Bonham's booming voice interrupted Jack's thoughts and rose above the hum in the room. "And then we can forget about inspections altogether I hope and get on with our school life!

The first is that, as from next term, St Cuthbert's *will* have computers on our premises and we *will* be studying information technology. Hang on, hang on!" he shouted, holding up his hands to quieten the cheer that came from the boys. "Computers will ONLY be used for creative projects and for learning. They will NOT, here at St Cuthbert's, be used for games. And that's not because we're mean!" he said, to counter the groans that rose from the hall. "It's because you can do that at home. If we don't keep space here for real life experiences and outdoor learning and play, well, we won't be St Cuthbert's anymore, will we!"

Many of the parents nodded at this.

"But we do need to keep up with technology," Mr Bonham went on, "and I include myself in that. I've realised, from studying my own computer records..." and here he looked at Jack, whose face instantly reddened – *he knows!* – "...And also from recommendations in the inspection report, how very important this is."

More polite clapping and nodding from parents.

"My second announcement," he went on, "concerns a boy here in this hall. One who only joined us this term and is now due to leave."

Jack's face flamed red again as heads turned in his direction and excited whispering rose from the hall. He was the only boy who joined this term! But what was Mr Bonham going to say?

"Jack Elliott, will you come out to the front please?"
What the?

Jack slowly got to his feet as Ellie nudged him in the ribs with her elbow and his mum said *Go on Jack, go up*. The excited whispers grew louder and the nudges bigger as he made his way to the end of the row, face burning, and then up onto the stage.

Oh... A lot of people!

The hall quietened.

"We don't need to go into detail here," said Mr Bonham, "but I've talked to a lot of the boys and to Mr Kay and other staff. And, even if the inspection news had not been good today, everyone is in agreement that Jack was a very, very important part of trying to help it go well."

There were whoops from the audience.

"So I would like to say a special thank you to you, Jack, for what you have contributed this term."

"Go Jack!" someone shouted.

"You are someone with a lot of creative ideas," Mr Bonham continued, "and many of them are very good ones that solve real problems."

In spite of himself, in spite of his burning face and staring at the floor, Jack felt himself starting to smile.

"And if some of those ideas have been a bit... well, controversial shall we say, we can overlook that this time, because they were all to good purpose."

Jack looked gratefully up at Mr Bonham.

And that was when he saw Rupert Woolacroft, sitting at the side of the stage with about twenty other visitors, mainly older men. *The Board! The old pupils!*

He stared, forgetting for a moment he was in front of everyone else, as he took in the different looking men: one with a grey beard and flamboyant neck scarf; quite a few in plain dark suits; another in sports wear; another in jeans and a shirt, in a wheel chair; and another in tweeds. Rupert Woolacroft, his face as brown and lined as Jack remembered it, was wearing slightly smarter clothes than when Jack last saw him, and no apron. He smiled broadly and gave Jack a big thumbs up.

"So, three cheers for Jack everyone, who has helped the school and found out one of the things he is good at, at the same time. Let us wish him luck in whatever he does in the future. Hip hip…"

"Hooray!" echoed the audience.

Jack couldn't believe it!

"Hip hip…"

"Hooray!"

Jack caught the gaze of some of his friends: Charlie, Vinnie, Wilf…and he laughed.

"Hip hip…"

"Hooray!"

Jack felt very, very… what was it?

He felt very, very *happy*.

~ ~ ~ ~ ~

The rest of the afternoon rushed by. Cases and boxes and bags and musical instruments, all packed the day before, were brought down by everyone, all at the same time, so the stairs and hallway and front drive were just a mass of moving, jostling baggage with heads appearing just above. Jack had more than most, as he carried his duvet and towels and everything that needed to go back with him; his wetsuit, as yet unused; his shorts and things for warmer weather, never needed.

Outside on the gravel driveway, bags and cases were quickly loaded into waiting open cars and doors were slammed. There were cries of *Hang on I've forgotten my washing*! Or *Wait! I need to say good-bye to Ed!* And *Have a great holiday!! Good-bye! See you next term!"*

Jack turned to his mum.

"This is it Jack," she said. "Time to go."

"Can I really not come back, Mum? Not at all?"

"I've spoken to Mr Clipper, Jack. He's kept your place open at Kerry Road. They're expecting you back."

"But Mum…" Jack felt overwhelmed suddenly by all he needed to say. "I just can't leave yet! There's loads I haven't done. Or found out. I mean, I know I'm good at ideas and all that now, but there might be other things. There will be. And I need to find them out!"

"I know… but we had a deal Jack. I only ever said a few weeks, remember?"

Jack scuffed at the gravel with his shoe. He remembered.

"And besides, we've missed you. I have, and Ellie has."

Ellie was chasing Zoe around the grass beyond the cars and didn't seem *so* bothered.

Jack sighed and looked around at the happy boys, leaving but knowing they were coming back. He would probably never see any of them again. And he hadn't even said goodbye to some of them! Well, he'd managed Charlie and Vinnie and swapped addresses. But what about Wilf and Zed?

Zed! Where IS he?

With a guilty pang, Jack realised he hadn't seen him at all, all day. In the excitement of seeing his mum and Ellie again, and having tea together, and hearing Mr Bonham's speech, he'd never managed to go and look for him. And just when he was about to, Rupert Woolacroft had come over to ask him about his weeks at the school. This had led to stories about when he and Mr Bonham were at St Cuthbert's – brilliant stories about scrapes they had got in to and challenges they had taken up – including one where the two friends had dared each other to climb the roof beams of the school hall...

"Did you... do anything while you were up there?" Jack had asked, thinking suddenly of teatime on his first day: the warm scones, the noise, and the letters RJW and SB scratched onto the roof beam above him.

Rupert Woolacroft smiled. "Is that still up there? Well, well..."

But now, Jack thought about Zed all over again. Where was he? Were his parents even here?

He looked around, searching the crowds for a black top hat or a cloak. But nothing... until, yes, there he was! At the side of the school building, hiding behind the wall. What was he doing?

But Jack knew straight away. He was watching all the children and families packing their cars and heading off for home. His parents clearly hadn't come. He had such a look of longing on his face that Jack was almost embarrassed to have seen it. Poor Zed. He must be so happy about the inspection news, knowing he would not have to move. But Jack had forgotten to think that he might also be sad today, stuck in school while everyone went away.

And through the whole experience of St Cuthbert's, he had strangely come to like Zed, for all his prickliness and sarcasm and not joining in.

"Mum," Jack said, on a sudden impulse, turning to her and Ellie where they now waited by the car. "Can I ask a really big favour?

"It really depends on what it is Jack."

"Nothing bad. It's just... could I maybe have someone back for the holidays? Or for some of it," he added quickly, seeing she was about to say no. "We could come back and get him later in the week?"

"Well..."

"He hasn't got anywhere to go, Mum. His parents didn't come and get him."

"Oh well then," she softened. "Of course you can ask him. If he's your friend."

Jack paused. *Was he?* And then he nodded. "Yes, he's my friend."

"But where will he sleep Jack? We don't have much room, remember?"

"That's not a problem," Jack smiled. "I just know he won't mind our house being small or cramped. I think he'll even kind of like it."

"Well okay...Hey! Hang on!" she called, as Jack set off at a run. "Where are you going?"

"To tell him!" he called back over his shoulder. "And I need to do something else too. Something important. Really quickly! I wont be long!"

And then, as he got nearer, calling ahead to where Zed stood.

"Hey Zed! Got something to ask you!"

~ ~ ~ ~ ~

In the trees, away from the school, everything was quiet. Jack and Zed stood under the big oak tree and stared up at the Den. It was just... the best.

"I need to thank you Jack," said Zed. "It was me who was dreading St Cuthbert's closing but it was you who did something about it. I was so relieved today. But now it's you who wont be coming back."

"I know." Jack put his hand out and touched the huge trunk. "It's not fair. It's going to be so different back at Kerry Road. You're lucky you can stay here."

"Well, in some ways," Zed said. And then, a little awkwardly, "Thanks for inviting me to your house. No one's ever invited me back before. And I wasn't exactly friendly to you for a while."

"That's okay," said Jack, generously. "It'll be cool if you come. We can play computer games!"

"Remember," Zed smiled. "I'm a Master! You have no chance. But it'll be good to come. And besides, I've never been to a house that doesn't have its own grounds before."

"Shut up!" Jack hit him, but he knew he was joking.

"Anyway," a gleam lit up Zed's face, under the angle of his top hat, and he gave Jack a nudge. "Come on then! I thought we were here so you can end your St Cuthbert's days in style!"

Jack smiled, as excitement returned. "You sure you don't want to join me?"

"I can't imagine anything I would less like to do. But please, go ahead."

Jack laughed. He turned and grabbed the swing and pulled himself onto the seat. He paused for a moment, seeing so clearly suddenly his dad's smiling face. Then he swung back and out a few times, taking in the Den, the woods ahead of him, the golden leaves, the sky, everything…

And then, at the highest point possible, with a whoop of excitement and daring and pure lovely happiness, Jack let go.

And he flew.

Printed in Great Britain
by Amazon.co.uk, Ltd.,
Marston Gate.